X Marks the Spot

Kit Barrie

Contents

Chapter One

My name is Jamie Davis, and this is my story. The circumstances of my childhood are not happy ones, nor are they uncommon ones. My mother was a local seamstress in the portside city of Brittlecreek, and my father was a sailor by trade. My mother passed from illness when I was still in leading strings. My father was always traveling the seas, so I was sent to live with my Uncle Nedry, who worked for the local shipbuilder as an assistant.

My time with Uncle Ned was beneficial, in that I learned to read and write, something that neither of my parents could do. Uncle Ned was a confirmed bachelor, and his employment created a modest but comfortable living for us. I thought that perhaps I would one day follow in his footsteps and become a shipbuilder myself, or sail the seas like my father. Neither was to be; at least, not in a recognizable way.

When I was nine, a terrific storm capsized the vessel my father was on, leaving me without parents. I would never forget the cry of anguish from

Uncle Ned when the port authorities came to tell him my father was lost, for my father had been his only remaining relative besides me. Uncle Ned then threw himself into raising me as a stalwart and honourable young man, and I presumed our lives would continue as they had.

On the eve of my fourteenth birthday, Uncle Ned was arrested for embezzlement, which I knew to be patently false, as he was a model of honesty and charity. But despite his pleas to the contrary, he was found guilty and transported for life, and all of his assets were seized, including the only place I had to call home. The local constabulary decided that, rather than sending me to a workhouse for orphans, my reading and writing skills could be turned into profit, and I was sold as a ward and indentured servant to Squire Harrington, a local dealer of antiquities.

Squire Harrington was an older man, a recent widower who had lost his wife of over forty years. They had never had children, and I admit that I had hopes that he would see me as more than an apprentice or ward. My time with Uncle Ned had given me a sense of family that I yearned for again, as my life had been turned upside-down in a matter of days. I lived with the squire, his lodgings being above the antiquities shop. He had a maid in once a week to give the place a cleaning and to prepare a hot meal for him, but otherwise, most of the work he left to me.

He was a kindly man, soft-spoken, no more bravery than a field mouse, with a curly, white wig that he wore under his slightly shabby tricorn hat. Nearly everything he owned was out of date, out of fashion, and mended or covered with patches. I discovered, when I was tasked to get the household accounts in order, that despite owning his own shop, Squire Harrington was terrible with money. He was as disorganised a man as one could ever find. He was also much too kind for his own good, lending money to friends in need and not getting it properly repaid to him. Through snippets of conversation and various letters and papers, I was also able to discern that he and his late wife had never been particularly well-endowed when it came to finances. Her mental and physical decline had taken its toll on the running of the household in her last few years, and he had fallen far behind on his bills and taxes. His grief at losing her had also produced in him a sort of melancholy where he was often unable to rouse himself from his bed, leaving his shop unopened, which did not help his financial state.

As such, I discovered that the squire had accumulated debts far beyond what his shop would be able to provide for. My heart ached as I realized that the kindly older man was positively drowning under the weight of financial obligations that he had no way of ever repaying with his limited means. It seemed unfair that someone who was so generous and good would struggle so much. He had used his meager funds to take me in to help him, which spoke without words of his desperation to get his life organised. Despite the grief of losing my uncle, I made it my goal to do whatever I could to help the old gentleman in any way I was able.

He was the sort of man who never raised his voice, even to scold me if I did something foolish. The only time I ever was afraid around him was when I was sixteen, and he found me out behind the shop with the butcher's son, our hands down each other's trousers as we shared clumsy, wet kisses. The other boy had fled, and I stood, trembling, afraid that Squire Harrington would strike me, or worse yet, send me away.

Imagine my surprise when he led me inside and told me that my lust for the same sex was understandable, and he would not discourage my proclivities, only warned me to be more discreet. Buggery was illegal, and the sentence was transportation. While I was not afraid of what might happen if I were transported to a new land, I was not ready to give up my life in Brittlecreek, and, still being a child, I was concerned with how I would make a living if I were to lose my position with the squire. And my apprehension for what the squire would do without me solidified my resolve to be more cautious with my explorations of these strange feelings that were making themselves known to me.

Squire Harrington found use for my education, having me catalog and organise some of his various collections. I was learning about different ages in history, from the time when the land was populated by giant reptilian creatures, to some of the civilizations across the sea that still existed today. Squire Harrington dealt in all types of artifacts, from fossils to coins, ancient clothing and jewelry, rudimentary tools, and all manner of writings. His knowledge was quite extensive, and it was through his teachings that I gained my love of history, architecture, and archeology. For my seventeenth birthday, he gifted me a fine silver compass on a chain. It was the first thing I had owned that was truly mine besides the clothing on my back, and I kept it hidden under a loose floorboard in my room, when I was not wearing it about my neck, like a "dandy peacock," as the squire would tease me.

I was not entirely sure if when I came of age I would stay on with him or find a use for these passions I was developing. But when my eighteenth birthday came and went, the squire made no mention of me leaving, other than to say that I could now do as I pleased, and if I wanted to find another trade, he would wish me all the best. I chose to stay.

Chapter Two

It was one day not far into my eighteenth year when Squire Harrington traveled out of town for several days with his carriage, leaving me in charge of the shop. When he returned, he had a man with him. The man couldn't have been older than the squire, but his face was haggard and looked like it had weathered many a rough day and night. His curls were thick and gray, hanging in scraggly tendrils about his sunken eyes and hollow cheeks. He shivered in the carriage, despite being wrapped in a mass of blankets that nearly doubled his size around.

Squire Harrington introduced him as George, an old friend of his, and said that George would be staying with us for the foreseeable future. I wondered to myself how long that might be, as the poor man looked like he could drop dead at any moment. His coat was of such patches that I could not tell what color it might have originally been. He had a large sea chest with him that the squire put in one of the spare rooms above the shop.

George spent most of the time in his room, staring out the window, muttering occasionally to himself and peering about with an old spyglass that looked as though it had seen as many rough days as he had. He was a very silent man by custom, until he had the spirits about him. The first time he ever addressed me, it was in a tottering voice that sent a shiver up my spine, as if someone had walked over my grave. "Boy," he creaked. "Be a good lad an' fetch ol' Georgie a drink of rum, woulja now?"

I presently fetched him a bottle, with the squire's permission, and George ignored the glass I brought in favor of swigging directly from the bottle, which he clutched in both his withered hands. I recall him to be one of the most prolific drinkers I was ever acquainted with; how the squire always managed to have enough rum about to satisfy him, I will never know.

Much of his time was spent drinking, and when he became drunk, he was quite the storyteller, though whether his tales were truth or the product of his own fraught mind was entirely up for debate. He told me he was a former sailor and had spent his life on the ocean, starting "when I were no more'n a weevil half yerh size." By his own account, he must have lived his life among some of the wickedest men that God ever allowed upon the sea. He had tale upon tale of fighting the king's soldiers, which I deemed were mostly true, and yarn upon yarn of meeting beautiful mermaids and other creatures of the deep, which I deemed were mostly not.

Our evenings, which had once been quiet, were now often filled with stories from George Conley, and those not filled with stories were filled with him banging away at the squire's wife's old spinet, slightly out of tune, singing at the top of his feeble lungs,

"A man at sea needs wind and rum,
So storms he can confront.
A man on land needs rum and gold,

So he can buy a c-"

"George!" the squire would interrupt him with a pointed look in my direction, and George would make an apologetic bow toward me that would almost topple him off the bench.

I asked Squire Harrington why George was staying with us, if perhaps he had family who would be wondering after him. But the squire merely shook his head and told me that George had no one from his former life who could be trusted to look after him. He told me that he had met George years ago when the man lived at an inn along the coast. George had once been a pirate, Squire Harrington told me, as if revealing a great secret. A first mate and trusted advisor to none other than the great pirate captain, Charles Locke.

I knew the name Charles Locke; there was hardly a soul in the land who did not. He had been one of the most notorious and vicious pirates to ever sail the seas. His reign of terror had lasted for a number of years, though he was dead now. He had been caught by the king's fleet, and he and the crew that were on board were sentenced to hang for piracy. The day he stood on the trap door at Execution Dock had been like Christmas for the townsfolk, the feasting and parading going on all day and all night. I had always thought it in poor taste to celebrate the demise of anyone like that, but both Uncle Ned and Squire Harrington had told me that I had a remarkably soft heart.

I wondered how George Conley had managed to escape the hangman's noose, so one day, when he seemed to be in fine spirits and about as sober as he probably could actually get, I asked him.

"Jamie, Jamie, Jamie," he said, patting my shoulder. "Pirating ain' no job fer an old man, an' I were older than the cap'n by a good amount o' years. I took me leave uh them, and good timing too, fer weren' more-an six months later that Cap'n Locke was in the ground, God ress his soul." He slapped his hand upon his chest in a show of respect that might have honoured his former captain if not for the great belch that accompanied it.

I had never been on a ship, let alone a pirate vessel, but I suspected that life on the seas was rough. My father was proof of that, as were the hundreds of deaths that occurred every year amongst sailors, whether pirate, merchant, or soldier. I didn't know if George had been as much of a drunkard aboard Captain Locke's ship, but if he had, he certainly would not have lasted much longer at any rate. I had never seen a man able to put away an entire bottle of rum the way George did, and I was surprised every morning to find him awake and tucking into his breakfast with the relish of a man ne'er had a drop in his life.

While friendly to the squire and I, George kept his eye on every person who came into the shop from his perch at the window that overlooked the front door. I asked him only once if he was looking for someone in particular, and he rounded on me with such a fury that I almost sprinted for the stairs. When his mood was no longer soured, he apologized, gave me a coin to buy myself a cross bun, and told me, "There be a score of men out there ta fear, Jamie, my boy. Always best ta keep a weather-eye open. If anyone comes a-pokin' 'round lookin' fer ol' Georgie, you let him know, an' there'll be another coin for yer troubles."

If anyone was looking for George Conley, I was unaware of it, until one fateful afternoon not so long into the spring. The cobbles were cold and wet with puddles, and the squire had gone out to meet with a buyer. The streets were deserted, save for a few souls hurrying through the misty rain in search of better accommodations. I stood at the counter, sorting through a pile of glass beads, when George poked his head around the doorframe of the shop, hissing softly to me. "Jamie..."

"What is it?" I asked, glad for a moment of respite as I stretched my neck out.

George had a piece of paper clutched tight in his hand, and I recognized the envelope it was in as having arrived earlier that day with our three-times-a-day post. When I turned to look at him, I found myself unsure of what I was seeing at first before realizing that he was staring sober at me, the expression of his face one of mortal sickness and terror.

George held up the paper which shook so badly in his hand that I had to grab his wrist to hold him still to take it. It was a scrap of parchment, with no adornments other than a large circle of black that had been drawn with ink onto the center of it. On the back, in a very good, clear hand, was written, "Dead men tell no tales. Nine tonight." This caused me to glance up at our old clock to see that it was just now half-past four.

"What is this?" I asked George, for his face had gone paler than the paper, making his dark eyes flash with madness that did not come from rum.

"The black spot," he rasped. "They're coming for me. Tonight."

"What is the black spot?" I asked, trying to break into the panic that seemed to be overriding him.

"A pirate's death sentence," George said, rushing forward to the shop door and flinging closed the lock, upsetting a table full of snuff boxes in the process. He rushed back to me and grabbed me by the shoulder. "Come on, lad!"

I found myself yanked after him as he hauled me toward the stairs with a strength I did not know he possessed. He took the stairs two at a time, and I raced to keep up with him. In his room, I could see he had already been at some manner of packing, his odds and ends strewn about, his sea chest open wide. On the bed sat a curved cutlass, with a rusted blade.

George flung himself to the chest and yanked something from it, holding it out to me. "'Ere, Jamie. This is what they're afta. Take it, keep it safe!"

It was a packet of papers, wrapped in an oilskin covering to keep it protected from moisture. George waved it at me, and I hesitantly took it from him. I started to undo the straps that tied it closed, but George tossed his hand. "No time, no time!" he said. "They'll be watchin' me, lad. Take it, go ou' the back like yeh are runnin' an errand, and don' come back!"

My mind was spinning as I tried to process George's words. "Who is watching you?"

But George was frantically shoving things into his trunk with great haste before he suddenly sank to his knees, his face pressed against the bed as he struggled to breathe. In an instant, I was by his side. "George?" I asked, touching his shoulder.

He tried to shove me away, but it was as if his arm were an iron rod, and he turned his eyes to me in desperation. "Jamie," he moaned softly, and the sound was like that of a mournful dog.

"Let me help you," I said, trying to slide my arm under his shoulder, but he shook his head with great effort.

"No," he said, then a little louder and firmer, "No!"

His eyes met mine, and I felt myself go rigid under his intense stare. "Jamie, lissen," he said, and every breath sounded like it barely was able to escape his throat. "Lissen ta me, lad. Yeh're a good lad, been a right decent sort ta ol' Georgie." He grasped my shoulder in his gnarled fingers as his hand shook. "Look here. They're comin' for me, an' I ain't in no form ta daddle 'em again. But you... you and the squire been right ol' mateys to the end wif me. I gave the squire meh word that he could have the map when I go, and this'll rightly be the end o' me. Go fin' the squire. And neither of yeh come back, yeh hear me? Ol' George won't tell 'em, I'll take it to meh grave." He let out a tremendous wheeze, the light in his eyes dimming a bit, and I could see that he already had one foot in said proverbial grave as he sat there. "You go. But be wary, boy, for where there's gold there'll always be blood to follow, you mark that."

"I cannot leave you here if someone is coming for you," I said as I tried to make sense of his ramblings, but George let out a harsh, rattling laugh.

"This be meh end, Jamie lad. As good an endin' as I deserve. I'll take 'em ta Hell wif me if I can. Now go." George pinned me with a hard stare, his eyes even more glassy now. "Go." When I did not move, he summoned the last of his strength. "Go!" he bellowed with the ferocity of the pirate he once was, and I turned and ran from the room.

I tucked the packet absently into my shirt, mind racing as I tried to process what George had told me to do. Go out the back, find the squire. I grabbed a basket and a lantern from the kitchen before opening the back door of the shop, my heart thundering in my chest. I wondered if someone would come leaping out at me from the shadows, but nothing moved. I headed off down the alley, listening hard for the sound of breathing or footsteps, but I only sensed my own as I walked. Once I reached the main thoroughfare, with its flickering lamps, I felt a little better, for it would be harder for anyone to sneak up on me in the wider streets. I knew Squire

Harrington had gone to meet with someone on Easter Lane, so I turned in that direction, trying to maintain my casual air, though all I wanted to do was sprint into the foggy darkness.

I ran into the squire as he was walking back from his client's office. "Jamie!" he said, his eyes scanning over me with worry. "You look a fright, lad, what's wrong?"

I tried to explain, but my words kept getting in my own way until Squire Harrington pulled us into a shop and had a pot of tea brought that warmed me and quieted my nerves.

In as calm a manner as I could, I explained to him about George receiving something called the black spot and how he had told me to run and not return. The squire waited until I had finished my breathless retelling. Then he patted my shoulder and told me I did well, and that we would have to return to the shop in the morning, for we could not just abandon our home without warning. But there was a worry in his eyes I had not seen before. I thought it then to be concern for George's safety.

We stayed away from the antiquities shop, as George had instructed. If he feared the men as much as it seemed he did, we had good reason to not come under their scrutiny. We found a lodging house for the evening, and I tried to sleep, but it eluded me. I found myself wondering what happened to George. Was he all right? Had he rallied from his sudden fit? Had he died before the men even arrived?

The sky had barely started to show signs of the coming dawn when both Squire Harrington and I made our way back to the shop, neither of us having been able to sleep a wink. We were unsure what we would find, but that same thought drove us forward through the streets.

You cannot imagine a shop in such a state of smash. But for the sign over the door, you would not know what goods had once been hawked inside its walls. Countless trinkets scattered the floor in various states of ruin amongst the broken glass. Statues and sculptures had been decapitated or shattered entirely. The entire shop might have been picked up by a giant and shaken like a globe of water. There was no sign of habitation on the first floor.

Thoughts of self-preservation abandoned me, and I took the stairs two at a time, emerging onto the upper floor landing. The chaos from below had not prepared me for the nightmare that was above. While death was not uncommon in our lives, the level of violence that I knew had to have been enacted upon at least one person was entirely unfamiliar. Blood spattered the walls and even the hallway ceiling in great, streaked droplets, as if the artist had flung his brush of crimson madly about. The hallway furniture had been overturned in such a way that I had to clamber over it to make my way down the hall. I kicked something small as I walked in the dimness. I bent to pick it up, then dropped it with a ferocious cry as I realized it was a finger. Bony, the nail stained with dirt and blood, with a small tattoo of an anchor on it. I had no doubt it had belonged to George Conley.

A scrambling noise behind me made me jump, and I turned to see the squire making his precarious way over the makeshift barricade. He was carrying a lit lantern and had a pistol tucked into his belt, and he pulled it free once he was over the hall console. He examined the finger I had just dropped with a darkening frown. He gave me a nudge. "Stay behind me, Jamie," he said softly, and I was more than happy to oblige that request as we made our way down the hall. The blood spatter grew thicker the further we went until we reached the door of George's room, standing ominously ajar.

The squire pushed the door open and leveled his pistol, but there was not a living soul to be seen in the tiny room. There was, however, even more destruction, and what might have once been a man sprawled on the bed. The putrid smell of blood and rot hit us full in the face, and we both retched.

George Conley was most definitely dead. The fact that several pieces of his body had been separated from one another would have been enough indicator of that. Someone had tortured him, though why anyone would do such a thing was beyond my comprehension at the moment.

The squire let out a string of curses that I had never heard from his kindly personage before, enough that my ears burned red. The man shoved the lantern into my hands and suddenly was on his knees amidst the blood and carnage, digging through the remains of the sea chest at the foot of the bed. He flung aside everything he touched, and when he did not find what he was searching for, he flew about the room, looking in every drawer and under every piece of furniture, as I watched in dismay, unsure how to help but also unwilling to search amongst the gore myself.

The squire suddenly let out a cry as never heard from a man, sinking to his knees amongst the wreckage, his head in his hands, pulling his powdered wig from his head as if to see better. "Jamie," he moaned. "We are ruined, my boy. They've gone and taken it, and we are lost!"

"Taken what?" I asked, for while many of the antiquities below seemed unaccounted for, none of them had been of significant enough value that such a man as the squire would despair so mightily. And George certainly had not had much of value in his chest that I was aware of.

"The map," he said, his voice rough and grinding in his throat. "Old Locke's map."

I felt the lump inside my vest that I had entirely forgotten about in my panicked flight and present return to the slaughter. Its weight was heavier now with the memory of George Conley in it. I removed it from my shirt, holding it up for the squire to see. "Would this be the document in question?"

The squire lifted his head, and I have never seen a man look more astonished than he at that moment, as though the blessed Mother had appeared in front of his very eyes. He snatched it from my hands with such ferocity that the oilskin left a sting on my palms. He undid the bindings to reveal a parchment within, yellowed with time and salt air. Still on his knees, his hands shaking, he turned to look at me. "Jamie," he breathed. "Where did you get this?"

"George, he gave it to me," I said, suddenly wondering if perhaps I had done something I ought not to. "Before I left. He told me to take it and give it to you, like he had said he would."

Squire Harrington leaped to his feet with the agility of a man half his age, throwing his arms around me and spinning us in a mad circle while he shouted with joy. "We're saved! Oh, Jamie, we're saved!" he said, releasing me and doing a few steps of a jig. "You are brilliant, and you shall have all that you deserve!"

"Sir, I don't understand," I said, desperate to have some answers from him as his feet tapped on the wooden planks in a merry dance. "What is this?"

Squire Harrington stopped dancing and held up the document for me to see. "Do you remember I told you about Captain Locke?"

I nodded, still not understanding what I was meant to know.

The squire pointed to the corner of the parchment. Inscribed were 2 letters. C and L. "Charles Locke," he said. "He captured several frigates full of gold and treasures headed for the European mainland. But when he died, he had not a single coin on him. For many years, it was said that he buried his treasure on an island and planned to return one day to find it, and he created a map that showed the location of the treasure." The squire waved the document again. "This is that map!"

I still had so many questions, but the squire seemed beyond paying attention to me now, studying the chart with great intent. "We shall have to rent a ship and a crew, of course, of a trustworthy nature, but that should not be too hard. Long have I dreamed of a life at sea, though it would have been much better in my younger years. Oh, Jamie, what excitement we shall have!" And he did another dancing step before sobering amongst the remnants of what had once been George Conley. "Come, we must away to the docks."

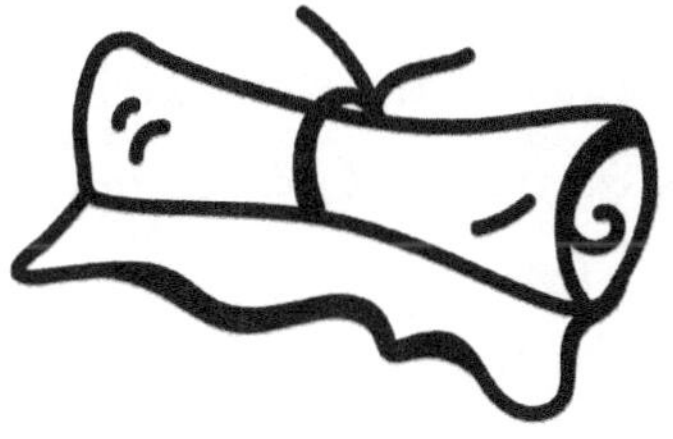

Chapter Three

We alerted the police about the break-in without mentioning the map or the black spot, which was nowhere to be found, and I assumed the fiends had taken it with them. The constables and coroner came to examine the scene of the crime. They all seemed to agree that it was a burglary gone wrong, and George had been unfortunate enough to encounter them as they raided the shop. Neither the squire nor I were inclined to correct this assumption. George's remains were taken away, and the squire and I packed a few items of clothing and things of significance. Most important to me, I grabbed the compass from under the floorboard in my room that had mercifully gone unnoticed, despite the rest of the room having been completely ransacked.

The squire paid several men to clean up the shop and the living quarters, and to box up all the antiquities that were salvageable. He told them we would be traveling for a long while, and that the key to the shop was to be turned over to his solicitor once the wreckage had been dealt with. And then we left.

We took the squire's carriage and horse, which had luckily both escaped the plundering, to the nearest seaport town of Highcastle. This, the squire informed me, was where he had found George those few months ago, full of drink and empty of pocket. George had recognized him, and after much conversation and libations, George had confessed to Squire Harrington that he had Captain Locke's map. "I ain' naught but a sea rat, wif no strength in me old bones. Yeh give ol' Georgie a place tah stay fer the winter an' a bottle-a rum when 'e has a thirst, an' he'll give you the map. 'T'weren' no good ta meh anyway, I'd be dead 'afore the anchor was weighed."

We found an inn close to the docks where we stayed, the squire selling his horse and carriage for the funds to stay in a modest but clean room and to have meals brought up from the tavern twice a day.

The squire was gone for much of our time there while I sat and studied the map behind the locked door. The island was not overly large. There was a river that ran through it, and some labeled rock caverns upon its western bank. There was a bay to the south that was listed as being the ideal location for landing a ship. And in the upper northeast corner of the island, a bright red X had been made, toward the very edge of the line that delineated island from ocean. There were some instructions written to the side of it, a little smeared, as if someone had touched them with damp fingers, but I was able to make them out.

Bend in the river, bearing to a point of N.N.E.
Old Hawk points the way to the N.W.
The ridge to the north
Seek within, 162 paces.

These instructions were maddeningly vague, but I suspected they would make more sense upon reaching the island in question, whose coordinates were laid out in another corner of the map.

With the remaining funds he had, Squire Harrington met with another of his old friends, one Kearns by name, striking some sort of bargain I was not privy to, and within a week, he had secured us a ship, getting her by the most admirable management for the merest trifle. Squire Harrington met with the captain of the ship and was delighted by him, inviting him to the inn to talk with us.

I sat at the table in the corner of the tavern, near a roaring fire, drinking some terrible concoction that might have been ale. The weather was warming now, and the tables were filled with all manner of men, many of whom were new to Highcastle, seeking jobs on ships now that seasonal travel was not hampered. The squire had just finished tucking into a large bowl of rabbit stew when the captain walked in, and the squire rose from his seat to wave him over.

The captain was a tall man, taller than the squire by a good several inches and much taller than myself. He carried himself with confidence, his chin lifted high, his back straight. He was currently dressed in a fine linen shirt, waistcoat, and dark trousers, red silk cravat at his throat, with shiny black boots on his feet, and a silk scarf with some of the finest embroidery I had ever seen wrapped around his waist. His hair was short and dark, his eyes the color of melted chocolate drops, and a fine bristle of hair covered his strong jaw. He was probably of late twenties in age, and I might have pegged him for a dandy rather than a seafarer if not for the single ring of gold he wore in his right ear. He smiled, ignoring the few curious or appreciative looks from the inn patrons he received as he strode across the room to us, holding out his hand for the squire to shake. "Good to see you again, Squire." His voice was deep and flowed elegantly. Then his eyes turned to me, and I am rather ashamed to admit that my breath caught in my throat. "And you must be young Mister Davis."

He held out his hand, and I took it with my own that trembled slightly, for I had never seen a man such as this. His smile was as bright as the midday sun, and his fingers around mine were warm and firm. "Yes, sir," I managed to squeak out, and the man laughed heartily and gave my hand a solid shake.

"Miles Ambrose, Captain, at your service," he said, spreading his arms to the side and giving a slight bow, like an actor after a performance.

"Captain Ambrose crews the MORAY, which we have engaged for our expedition," Squire Harrington said. "And he has a fine vestment of crew members as well."

"Indeed I do, sir," Ambrose said, sitting down at the chair the squire proffered, close enough to me that his knee touched mine under the table. "Seeking a few more solid hands before the mast, but we shall be ready to ship out before the end of the week."

The squire nodded, swiping at his forehead with his handkerchief. "I trust your judgement thus far, Captain, your help has been invaluable."

Ambrose gave him that bright smile before turning to me, and I felt my cheeks warm as I gazed back into his dark eyes. "The squire says you have never been to sea before, lad."

"I... I have not, sir," I said, my voice catching in my throat and making me swallow to get it out. "But my uncle was a shipbuilder, so I am familiar, at least."

"Excellent," Ambrose said, his voice a purr that sent a strange heat through my chest and stomach, down to my toes. "I am certain we can find a great use for you, Mister Davis, and I would be pleased to take you under my wing to teach you about seafaring."

His knee pressed a little harder against mine under the table. At first I thought it might be a mistake, but then it pressed again, and I felt the brush of his booted foot against mine. I knew my cheeks were pink as I said, "I would be pleased to learn under you, Captain."

Ambrose laughed again, the sound richer than any dark wood or brocaded silk. "Then so you shall, lad, then so you shall!" And we drank to our upcoming voyage and good fortune.

Chapter Four

The sky was clear, the air breezy the day we were to set sail. Though I had lived by the shore all my life, I had never been near the sea till then. We climbed up the gangplank of the MORAY, which was as fine a vessel as the man who captained it. Polished wood and brass, white sails, the deck freshly scrubbed. Mister Kearns was already aboard, having decided through some arrangement with the squire to accompany us on our journey. I did not know the particulars of his dealings, but I suspected the squire had promised him a share of the treasure in exchange for his help in finding the ship.

"Well, gentlemen," he said as we stepped onto the ship's deck. "Are you determined to go on this cruise?"

"Like iron," answered the squire, and I could see the glint of gold in his eyes and the eyes of Mister Kearns.

The squire had advised me not to talk about the purpose of our expedition or the existence of Captain Locke's map to anyone; he had taken possession of the packet with the charts before we boarded, and my compass was safely stowed amongst my belongings in my small cabin alongside the squire's. The room was furnished with only the barest of necessities, but I figured I would not spend much time in it, anyway. I was to have a job on board the ship as an assistant to the cook and the officers.

The first mate's name was Humbolt, and he was a man of cadaverous thinness and skin the color of a tallow candle. He spoke few words, but when sea shanties were sung, he was amongst the loudest and most enthusiastic of singers. He showed me around the ship, and I drank it all in like a thirsty man drinks water, every piece of rope or fixture or embellishment a treat for my soul that had been locked to land for my eighteen years, despite the call of the sea from my father and uncle.

Once we had surveyed the world above deck, Humbolt led me down a set of stairs into a room filled with more darkness than furniture, to an area that smelled heartily of root vegetables and spices. "The galley," Humbolt said in his ragged tone, waving a hand around. "And this is our ship's cook." A form materialized from the shadows, hulking and moving in a way that sent my skin prickling.

The man was older than I, and even older than Captain Ambrose by more than a few years, perhaps in his late thirties. It was hard to tell from the scars that dug trenches into his face, aging him beyond his years. At one time he might have been a handsome fellow, but it was obvious life had beaten him down more than once.

His skin was a deep brown, almost black, and the sun had not been kind to his ruddy cheeks and forehead. He had a large, flat nose that looked like it had been broken at some point, and his hair was so short that it was almost not there. He was a barrel-chested man, with wide shoulders and waist. He had scars that carved gashes into what at one time must have been smooth skin on his cheek, the side of his mouth, and the corner of his left eye, making it droop slightly.

His unnatural movement was understandable, as I saw now that he only had one leg. His left leg was almost entirely missing, his loose trouser fabric tied up to a stump that, at one point, had been the top part of his thigh. Despite the missing limb, he stood easily on his single good one, leaning lightly on his crutch, though it seemed like he could stand fine even without it. His broad shoulders hunched, making him appear shorter than he actually was. If he had been standing straight, I had no doubt he would have been a good foot taller than I, and more than twice as broad.

"Cross. Silas Cross," the giant said, holding out one large hand. I took it hesitantly, and he closed his fingers in a firm grasp, giving it a hearty shake. I thought he might be smiling at me, but the twist of his mouth under the scars made it difficult to tell.

"Jamie Davis. It's nice to meet you, Mister Cross," I said. His hand was rough and calloused in mine, nearly encompassing it.

Silas Cross let out a soft rumble of laughter from deep in his chest. "No need for formality, Mister Davis. Yeh can jus' call me Silas."

"Then you may call me Jamie," I said with a polite smile. I wasn't sure how I felt about this large man yet. Something about him unnerved me, though I could not place a finger on it. I had seen men scarred and wounded before; they were not unusual to see in Squire Harrington's shop, often selling their few remaining trinkets for no more than a mouthful of food or a shot of brandy. But this man was to be my comrade for the foreseeable future, and I was not about to be impolite or start off our relationship on a bad note. "What may I do to help you, Silas?"

Silas glanced at Humbolt, who silently headed back up the stairs, leaving me with the one-legged hulk of a man. He inclined his head at the table he had been sitting at nearby, peeling potatoes and turnips. "If yeh'd be so kind."

I nodded and took a seat on the bench there. Silas followed after me, moving easily around the galley, unhampered by his missing appendage. He picked up another knife before he came and sat on the other end of the bench, handing it to me. I took it, then watched him pick up his own knife and begin to peel the potatoes with surprising speed and dexterity. The light through the boards above us and the nearby lantern's glow caught his blade's edge and made it glint. The potatoes looked like nothing more than river stones in his hands. I noticed as he cut that he also was missing the two furthest fingers on his left hand, but he still easily held the potatoes and worked the blade around them.

I had not meant to stare, but he obviously knew I was as he commented, without looking up from his work, "I was a member of the Royal Navy, no' so many years ago now. Go' into a fight wif a long nine and lost."

I blinked, feeling my face go red. "Oh," was all that I was able to say.

"Lost my whole company in tha' battle," Silas said, still not looking my way. "Those tha' were left after disease took its toll, tha' is."

I didn't know what I could possibly say to his trite tone, so I managed, "I'm sorry," though what I was sorry for remained unclear in my own mind.

Silas nodded, still not looking up from his work. "War is hell, Jamie. Avoid it if ever yeh can."

"Yes, sir," I said softly, picking up my own knife. We continued the work in uncomfortable silence for a long time after that.

The first time I saw Captain Ambrose on the ship, he was dressed in his fine linen again, but now he had a beautiful black coat with white and silver trim adorning it, and a black tricorn hat to match. If ever a man looked to be a captain, it was Miles Ambrose. If I had seen a king or an archbishop, I could not have been more delighted. He stood on the upper deck by the helm, gazing out to the sea with a brass spyglass. I could not help but stare as the sun caught the silver buttons on his coat and made them glimmer like diamonds. He turned his head, and when he saw me, he gave me another of those smiles that warmed me from my head to my feet. He was extraordinarily handsome, and if I had ever had a doubt in my life that I was attracted to men rather than women, Captain Miles Ambrose crushed that doubt with a single glance. I smiled back at him, and he held up his hand and curled his fingers, gesturing for me to come join him. My heart stuttered in my chest, and I nearly took the stairs two at a time in my haste.

"Jamie, lad!" he greeted, putting his black-draped arm around my shoulders. "It is good to see you again."

"And you, Captain," I said, his arm warm and heavy around me. While I had been embraced before, something about this gesture from Ambrose felt more intimate than those of others.

"Care to have a look?" he asked, holding the spyglass out to me. "There are some dolphins not too far out."

I took the spyglass and stepped to the railing, holding it up against my eye. Indeed, there were several dolphins leaping out of the water at not a great distance, splashing delightedly as the sun caught their slippery skin. I had never seen dolphins before, only read about them, and I laughed as they dove and leaped in the waves.

And then suddenly Ambrose was behind me, his hands resting on the railing on either side of where I stood. I could feel the warmth and the brush of his coat against my back, though he was not pressed against me, and I nearly dropped the spyglass. My cheeks and ears suddenly burned, and I shifted a little as the proximity of the handsome man sent a rush of desire through me, down my back and into my trousers. I held the spyglass to my eye with shaking hands at the unfamiliar sensation, then felt Ambrose's warm breath ghost over my ear. "Aren't they magnificent?"

"Y... Yes," I said, the wind stealing the word from me as my sandy blond hair whipped around my face.

"I could stand here and watch them all day," Ambrose said, not moving, but I felt myself lean into him just a little, the folds of his black coat brushing over my back.

"I could too," I said softly. I felt him shift just a bit, so he was pressed firmer against me. It only lasted for a moment, and then Ambrose stepped away from me toward the helm to speak with the sailor there. The wind gusted between us, and I forced myself to stare at the dolphins until the heat had left my trousers and my face.

Chapter Five

My first night at sea was a restless one, for I was unused to the rocking of the ship and the constant roar and splash of the waves. I was in the galley to help Silas prepare breakfast long before the sun crested the horizon. Our awkwardness from the day before seemed to have been forgotten, for this morning he was in a merry mood, whistling softly as he moved around, a jaunty sea tune I did not know. "How long were you in the Royal Navy?" I asked him when he took a pause in his whistling to swallow some water.

The laugh that rumbled inside of him was like the echo of a fired canon. "Longer than half me life," he said, handing a cup to me. "Was younger than yeh are now when I star'ed. 'Ad been near all over the worl' by the time I was twenty."

I tried to imagine seeing most of the world at such a young age, but it was beyond my comprehension. "What did you do in the Navy?"

"I started jus' like you, helpin' in the galley. But I learned real fas'. Fer a while I was a rigger, an' I learn'ta fight. Ain' so good with a pistol, but you give ol' Silas a blade, and 'e'll show 'em what's what!" He suddenly spun his cutting knife around his hand, swishing it through the air as if fighting invisible marauders, before he slammed it down with deadly accuracy in between two of the table planks where it stuck and quivered. I jumped, clapping my hands in excitement, and he gave me another of his bright grins.

"Did you ever fight pirates?" I asked breathlessly.

Silas let out one of his full-bellied laughs. "I did," he said. "Not as offen as yeh might think, but it 'appened a few times."

"Are there still pirates out there?" I asked, my mind suddenly drifting to the possibility that we might encounter such a vessel on our own voyage.

"Yes," Silas said, suddenly solemn. "Still qui'a few of 'em. But never yeh fear, Jamie. No pirate's gonna harm yeh wif Silas Cross around!"

When the time came for dinner, the squire, Mister Kearns, and Captain Ambrose were in the captain's private quarters, talking and smoking long, fine cigars. I knocked on the door of the cabin, and Ambrose opened it with a beaming smile that flushed me with heat as I pushed the cart of food inside. I had not yet been in the captain's quarters, or even seen any before, and I stopped short just inside the doorway. The room was beautiful, decorated with silk curtains and tapestries that I was sure were not made in England. The wood was all dark, highly polished, and skillfully carved. An elegant four-poster bed was in the corner with silk sheets on it. Everything was in a neat and tidy order. I could see that Captain Ambrose was a man of expensive and exquisite taste. I longed to run my fingers over the polished wood and plush cushions, so different from the older, faded pieces the squire had that had been out of fashion for more than twenty years now. Over by the desk was a perch, upon which sat a large blue and yellow parrot with a long, curved beak, who was cleaning his feathers but paused in his work to eye me curiously.

Ambrose caught me staring and laughed, gesturing for me to put the food on the desk. I did so, not taking my eyes off the brightly-colored bird who cocked his head almost upside-down to look at me. "This is Bosun," he said. "Say hello, Bosun."

Bosun clicked his beak and made a curious noise that sounded almost like, "Hello." Ambrose held up his hand, and Bosun gave a mighty flap to land on his arm, leaning in to give the gold ring on Ambrose's right ear a playful nip.

"He's beautiful," I said softly. I had never seen a parrot before.

"You can pet him," Ambrose said, offering his arm to me, and I tentatively reached out to stroke my fingers down the silky, tropical blue back. Bosun ruffled his feathers and let out a series of sounds that might have been some sort of attempt at speech, making me laugh.

Ambrose offered Bosun a bite of a cracker, and the bird took it in the talons of one foot, nibbling on it as he stared at me with his round, unblinking eyes. Ambrose gestured to the tray of food at the desk. "Come, Kearns, Squire," he said with his rakish smile. "And Mister Davis, you'll join us too, lad."

"I can't," I said, hearing the disappointment in my own voice. "I need to help Silas with the crew meal."

"Ah, yes, that Mister Cross," Ambrose said with a nod. "New to my crew, he is, but a good-hearted fellow. What do you think of him, Mister Davis?"

"I like him," I said, to which Ambrose turned his silver smile upon me, and I straightened up to my full height, which was still inconsequential compared to him.

"He does seem a good man, in spite of his injuries," the squire commented. He picked up something from the desk, and I saw that it was the oilskin packet with George Conley's map. He wrapped it up and carefully slid it into the inside pocket of his jacket before starting to serve up the meal.

"There's something about him I don't like," Mister Kearns said, heaping his own plate full.

"You think that about everyone," Squire Harrington said with a chuckle.

"And I have yet to be wrong," Mister Kearns said, to which the squire and Ambrose both laughed.

Chapter Six

Silas and I worked side by side daily in both companionable silence and extended bouts of camaraderie. While he was not pretty to look at, he had the most indomitable spirit. He was always ready with a joke or story, and I learned several rather bawdy sea shanties from him that would have made the squire blush if he had heard them from my lips. But while he was friendly and amiable, and had many tips about cooking and wilderness survival and sailing, Silas spoke very little about himself. This puzzled me a great deal, as most men are wont to brag about themselves from time to time, and I had told him my story, about losing my mother and father, and then my Uncle Ned, and coming to live with Squire Harrington. So one afternoon, as we sat peeling apples, I screwed up my courage.

"You said you were in the Navy for over half your life. Did you like it, to stay that long?" I asked.

Silas stared past me through the hull at something only he could see. "Fought, sailed, traveled the worl', them parts was all right. But I seen men blown to 'oly hell, an' I seen all kinds of things yeh ain' ever s'pose ta see. Gives me nigh'mares, it has, from time t' time. Fightin' ain' no life, Jamie Davis. Fightin' and killin' changes yeh, an' I don' ever wish to see tha' happen to yeh." He turned his dark brown eyes to me, looking frightfully solemn. "Yeh only ever kill if yeh have to. Leave the fightin' to men like me. Killin' takes a piece o' yeh're soul, and yeh're too good for that, yeh hear me?"

He stared at me with such intensity that my lungs constricted in my chest. "I hear you," I said.

Silas put his meaty hand on my shoulder and gave it an affectionate squeeze. "I tell yeh, Jamie. People will underestimate yeh, for all kin's o' reasons. Like if yeh're young, or if yeh got darker skin, or if yeh ain' educated same as them. But tha's when yeh prove 'em wrong, by God. Yeh're a wee thing, but yeh're tough."

I laughed at that, for I had never been referred to as "tough" by anyone. "I'm not," I said, shaking my head. "Not like you."

"I ain' say yeh're like me," Silas said, giving me one of his bright smiles that made his teeth gleam in the lantern light. "Thar's diff'ren' ways to be tough. Some folks got it in their hans. Some folks got it in their hearts. You gots it in yehr heart."

I smirked softly at that. "I don't suppose a tough heart will do any good if we encounter a pirate fleet."

"No'un, I don't suppose it would," Silas said with a chuckle. He held up his hands like a pugilist. "Try an' hit me."

"I don't want to hit you," I said. Despite knowing that Silas had trained for many years, it still seemed rather unsportsmanly to swing at a man with only one leg.

"Yeh scared?" Silas chuckled, waving his fists around playfully. "I'm twice yeh're size, lad, yeh ain' gonna hurt me now." He held up his right palm, tapping it with the remaining fingers of his left. "C'mon, hit righ' here."

I had never hit anything in my life, so I had no doubt I was about to make a great fool of myself. I balled up my fist and smacked it into Silas's palm. My knuckles smarted, though Silas's hand didn't move an inch, and I shook my hand out while Silas grinned at me. "I tol' yeh ta hit me." I gave him a playful glower. "I's jus' teasin' ya, lad, tha' weren' bad."

"Your hand is like a brick wall," I said, giving a suck to several of my knuckles.

Silas grinned and ruffled my hair. "Yeh're not much fer a figh', Jamie Davis. Bu' yeh's smart, an' that means a lot nowadays."

"Not smart enough not to hit you," I pointed out with a wry grin, and Silas's belly laugh echoed off the galley walls. "Why are you doing this, Silas?" I suddenly asked, a little surprised at my own temerity.

"Doin' what?" Silas asked, looking at me sideways. I wondered for a moment if he might be unhappy with my question, but his scarred face had not changed expression.

"Working as a cook," I said. "When you are so much smarter than that."

Silas grinned. "You flatterin' me, Jamie Davis?"

I rolled my eyes. "You said yourself, people will underestimate you. You could work in the royal office, or help train Navy sailors. Yet, here you are on a hired vessel, working in a galley. Why?"

Silas chuckled softly deep in his chest. "Tha's a fair question," he said thoughtfully. "I suppose it's cause I wanted ta go to sea again, and a good berth as a cook seemed a fine way to do it. And," he added with another rumble of laughter, "I likes to cook."

"You do?" I asked in surprise.

Silas nodded. "I know yeh wouldn't think it of me much to look a' me, but I learned how to cook from me da' when I was just a wee nipper. We din' have much money now, but what we did have he stretched to make some of the most amazin' meals yeh'd ever eat in your life. The things tha' man could do with a piece o' meat and a potato was like watchin' the Lord turn water inta wine. He taught me to cook fer our fam'ly, and when I was old enough, I helped him at his fish cart."

"He was a fisherman?" I asked curiously.

"No," Silas said with a hearty smirk. "'E had a stand next to the fish market by the docks. People could buy their fresh seafood a' the market and bring it to him, and 'e'd cook it for them. If'n they didn't have their own kitchen, like."

I smiled at that idea, of selecting fresh fish or a bowl of mussels and having someone else cook them for me with a passion that I did not feel when it came to making food. "Then why did you join the Navy if you liked cooking so much?" I asked.

Silas's scarred face fell just a little at that, his voice dropping lower inside of him. "Me da' died when I was fifteen. Me mum was gonna have another baby, an' I already 'ad two sisters. I weren't gonna be able to make enough money without me da' around to support 'em. So I joined the Navy. Had all the food and clothes I needed, so I could send my weekly pay home to 'em while me mum an' oldest sister did more o' the neighborhood mendin'."

I suddenly realized how fortunate I had been that the squire had taken me in, or I might also have ended up conscripted in the Navy like Silas had. Silas had been a boy, younger than me, when he was turned into a weapon. His passion for food and cooking had fallen by the wayside, and he had sacrificed that, as well as his body, for king and country, with nothing to show for it but his horrific scars and the nightmares that plagued him. "Do you regret it?"

"Regre' what?" Silas asked.

"Going into the Navy."

Silas was silent, giving my question more contemplation than I thought it deserved, before he said, "No, I don'. I ain' proud of everythin' I did, but I don' regre' it. I ain' much about livin' in the past. What ma'ers is the here an' now. An' fer now, I'm 'ere wif you. An' I gets ta cook, e'en if it ain' a gourmet meal."

"I think your cooking is fantastic," I said in full honesty, and Silas ruffled my hair again.

Chapter Seven

While my relationship with Silas was easy-going and comfortable, every time I saw Captain Ambrose, my stomach would tighten and my breath would catch in my throat. He was a man of poise and impeccable taste, with a learned elegance about him. He was not a man born to wealth and power, which led me to think he had acquired it in some way. If others were as entranced by him as I was whenever his dark eyes met mine, it would have been quite understandable.

When I was not helping Silas, I'd find reasons to be near Ambrose as he went about his duties on the ship. The rest of the crew were an odd bunch of fellows, some with a worn, haggard look about them, all of them a little rough around the edges. More so than I would have expected, considering Ambrose seemed to be a man of refinement. More than once, I overheard the crew laughing about how Ambrose was too big for his pockets, but then, almost none of them had more than two shillings to rub together, so I thought it may have simply been jealousy over his acquisitions.

Much of the crew tended to ignore me, young pup that I was in their eyes. A few made lewd comments or gestures toward the start of the voyage, but Ambrose heard about them, and while I don't know what happened, those actions toward me stopped. For that, I was quite grateful. The idea of being on a ship at sea with a bunch of burly men might have enticed some who favored that sort, but I was much too inexperienced and naïve to know what was authentic and what was not.

One thing I did know to be genuine was that Ambrose was always watching me when we were near one another. He found reasons to brush past me, just a little too close for it to be an accident, and I would feel the warmth from the swish of his coat and smell the salty sea air, enveloped in whatever expensive oil he had used on his person that day. The smile he gave me would warm me all the way to my toes, and I suspected I looked like a besotted schoolgirl when I would blush and duck my head.

Our first week of the voyage had us never alone, as Ambrose would often meet with the squire or Mister Kearns when he was not with the crew. But by and by, the novelty of being in his presence wore off for them, and sometime in the second week of our voyage, I delivered dinner to his quarters to find Ambrose entirely alone, save for Bosun perched on his shoulder, nibbling at the gold ring in his ear. He had not yet discarded his black jacket, only his hat, and his smile warmed me as I entered with the tray, which I placed on a nearby side table. He set aside the paper he had been writing on and motioned for me to come over to him. I did, my heart quickening in my chest.

On his desk was a map of the island, with the latitude and longitude marked out upon it, but it lacked the directions or the red X that indicated the treasure on the one the squire had. His fingers traced it idly as he gazed up at me. "I feel as if I have not had a moment's peace," he said.

"It's a big job, captaining a ship," I managed, giving him a smile that I knew was shyer than I meant it to be.

"It is," Ambrose said with a slightly dramatic sigh. "I am quite ready to be done with it."

"Done with it?" I asked in surprise.

Ambrose waved his hand around airily. "I don't care about a life at sea, Jamie. I'll be happy to settle on land, in a large house."

"With lots of closets for your fancy clothes?" I teased, and he grinned at me.

"Of course. I like the finer things in life," Ambrose said, before his hand slid up, and his fingers trailed lightly down my arm. Realizing we were alone in the room except for Bosun, the touch suddenly felt much more intimate than any other touch we had exchanged, and my cheeks warmed. I stepped back a few paces, wondering if I had broken out in a sweat as my skin prickled. And then my back hit the wall, pinning me in place under his gaze like a butterfly.

Ambrose rose from his chair, and Bosun hopped off his shoulder with a whistle, flapping onto his perch. "Dash my buttons, Jamie. Every time I look at you, I feel it like an arrow in my gut," Ambrose said, reaching up a hand to brush his fingertips lightly down my cheek. Certainly he took no pains to hide his thoughts, and certainly I read them like print.

My own breath caught as I stared up at him, licking my lips. I tried to form words, but they stuck in my throat like so much sugary candy. I felt my heart pick up several paces.

"Tell me," Ambrose said, leaning an arm over me, suddenly engulfing me in his shadow. "The squire I understand, but why are you here? What made you want to come along?"

"I..." My voice came out shaky, and I licked my lips again. "I suppose I have been wanting to explore the world, go on an adventure."

"Did you find the adventure you were looking for?" Ambrose purred, and suddenly his hips were pressed firmly to mine against the wall, the slight stubble of his afternoon shadow brushing the outside of my ear.

All ability to speak left me as his warmth enveloped me, and I felt the hardness in the front of his breeches press against my own through paltry fabric that suddenly seemed like both too much and not enough layers between us. His chocolate-brown eyes gazed into mine before he caught my chin lightly in his hand, as if about to reprimand me, before his lips pressed to mine in a searing kiss.

I had never kissed anyone besides the butcher's son before, and that had been a few inexperienced kisses that were more wet than pleasurable; this one was different. Ambrose's lips were soft, the touch of his hand on my face gentle but holding me quite firmly in place as the press of his mouth intensified. I let out a sound, not of protest, but surprise, my hands coming up to his black-coated shoulders, gripping the lapels that my scrabbling fingers found. He pulled back for just a moment, only enough for me to take a breath, before his mouth was on me again, harder, firmer, and I felt a gentle nip of his teeth on my lower lip. I jerked under him but was unable to move, my entire body pressed back against the wall and held in place by his. His hips suddenly ground against me, his pleasure obvious against mine, and my hips struggled to thrust back of their own accord.

One of his hands leaned against the wall to brace him as the one on my chin trailed down my throat, tracing over the collar of my shirtsleeves, before his fingers slid down my chest and found one of my nipples, rubbing his thumb over it through my shirt. I couldn't stop the moan against his mouth as a new sort of pleasure rocked through me. His thumb moved in little circles around the hardened nub, and each one made me squirm more than the last.

He finally broke the kiss between us but did not pull back, and I could feel his breath on my cheek. He suddenly grasped my nipple between his thumb and forefinger, giving it a pinch through my shirt, and I admittedly let out an undignified squeak. His laughter rumbled low in his chest, like the distant sound of thunder on the horizon. "Innocent as a newborn kitten," he teased, and my cheeks burned.

His hand slid down and grasped at my waist, tugging my shirtsleeves from my trousers so the shirt flounced and caught where our groins were still pressed together, before he reached up to undo the buttons of my waistcoat with more deftness than I would have expected from the refined man. The vest fell open and slid off my shoulders to the floor. And then his hand slid up under my shirt, trailing over my stomach with a touch that scorched my skin like hot coals before his fingers found my other nipple, and he brushed over that one too.

Pleasure shot through me, and I mewled, nearly knocking my head against the wall as I tipped it back. And then his mouth was against my neck, kissing it with feather-soft brushes as his fingers closed over my nipple and rolled it lightly. My hands still gripped his jacket, tugging fiercely as my inexperienced body shuddered with pleasure. He found a point near my collarbone and began to nibble it, his fingers switching to my other nipple, and I thought for a moment the floor might have fallen out from under me. I gave a moan, then realized how loud it sounded in the stillness of the cabin, and I quickly clapped my hand over my mouth.

Ambrose laughed and drew back from my neck, grabbing my hand and pulling it away. "No one will hear you, lad. The door is thick, and the sea covers a multitude of sounds."

My face colored bright pink at that, sure my freckles were standing out over the blush. Ambrose's fingers fell from my wrist to slide down my chest, stopping at my waist where our hips met and my shirt bunched. My need against his was aching, but I was unable to find the words for what I wanted, not even completely sure what I thought he might do. Ambrose's fingers found the lacing of my breeches, and he began to undo them. My heart picked up in my chest. He intended to take them off, something that I had not even had the opportunity to try with the butcher's son, or anyone else. He loosened the laces, then stepped back just a bit so he could get his hand in between us, his fingers sliding into the waist of my trousers, past my belly button and over my straining cock.

I gasped sharply, my hands sliding from his lapels up to grip the back of his neck. His fingers enclosed my shaft and started to stroke, ever so gently, as the hand supporting him against the wall came down to work my pants over my hips, and they slid down my legs to puddle around my bare feet. My fingers tangled into the soft, dark hair at the base of his neck, my face burning.

Ambrose suddenly pulled back, his warmth leaving me entirely. My shirt fell down, mercifully hiding my twitching cock under its folds, but I couldn't stop a moan of disappointment, my legs trembling a bit. "C... Captain?" I asked softly.

He smiled, and that dashing smile made my dick give a little surge under my shirt. "Miles," he corrected, one of his fingers tapping me on the tip of my nose like I was a pup before his hands went to his own jacket buttons. He removed the black coat and draped it over his desk, then pulled off the starched neckerchief at his throat, laying that aside too, and then his waistcoat, leaving him in just his shirtsleeves on top. His hand moved up to one of the buttons of his shirt, and my breath caught audibly in my throat. I had seen some of the crew shirtless, or even with less than that, but I had not seen Captain Ambrose looking anything other than fully polished and starched, like he had just come from the tailor's. His fingers paused at the top button. "What was that, Jamie?" he said with a small smirk that made me shiver.

I licked my lips, suddenly feeling like I had been standing in the hot sun for hours with nothing to drink. "I…" Words tried to form in my throat, but they did not connect to my brain, and I just stared mindlessly at him, my hands braced against the wall behind me.

Ambrose carefully undid the first button, and then the second, starting to reveal snatches of his sleek, muscular chest. "Yes?" he purred, pausing at the third button. "Another?"

I nodded silently, not sure my mouth would work, and he undid the third button, opening his shirt up to just below his pecs, the creamy tan of his skin showing through. My hands itched to rip open the last few buttons, my cock giving another eager jump under my shirt, but I stayed where I was, sure I looked like a landed fish with my staring eyes and open mouth.

"Hmm," Ambrose mused as he undid another button, and then another, and another, until his shirt gaped open, but not as wide as I had hoped to show off his musculature. He brought his hands up to fastidiously undo the buttons at the cuffs of his sleeves, each one taking a thousand years, I was sure. Once the cuffs were undone, without glancing at me, he toed off his boots and leisurely bent to put them side by side under the desk. The motion caused his shirt to gape wide, and I heard a small whimper come from my throat. It seemed he heard it too, because he smirked just a bit, but he did not look my way. He slid his shirt off and down his shoulders, folding it neatly on the desk with his coat before he turned to me, now wearing only his breeches. I gasped and felt my pink cheeks go scarlet as I took in his muscular torso, his arms sinewy and strong, his chest smooth and defined, with a dark patch of hair that started under his pecs and moved down his body to disappear into his trousers. The front of them bulged with his engorged cock, and my eyes kept drifting back to it even as I tried to drink in the sight of the rest of him.

Ambrose suddenly paced toward me, and before I could do much more than gasp, he had scooped me up in his arms, holding me like a child. I was curled against him, feeling his warmth, the salty tang of the sea on his skin tickling my nose like an exotic perfume. He carried me easily, as if I weighed no more than a doll, setting me down on one of his heavy, cushioned chairs. My shirt rode up a little, and he was suddenly kneeling in front of me, his hands on my bare knees. He pushed them apart, which made me slide down in the chair a bit, spreading me wide for him to look at. I blushed and gave a small wiggle as my knees tried instinctually to close, to hide myself from his scrutiny, but he only pushed them wider, lifting my knees up to drape them over the carved arms of the chair. The cool wood dug into my burning thighs, the sensation of having myself so exposed to someone both mortifying and exhilarating.

"You're so pretty, lad," Ambrose purred, his hand moving to push my shirt up my stomach, fully baring my torso. "Your ass would make angels weep."

The words tickled my skin like silk, and my cock gave another small jump. My hands held onto the chair arms as Ambrose's laughter rumbled close to my legs. And then suddenly he was between my thighs, and the head of my cock was in his mouth. I jumped as the unfamiliar but incredible wet heat enveloped me, letting out a sound that might have been an attempt at a curse but got stuck along the way. His lips closed around my shaft, and he sucked on me in a way that made white flickers dance in front of my eyes.

His mouth rocked further down on me, then back up again, and my moans began to follow the rhythm of his lips as they slid up and down, the tip of his tongue gliding up the underside of my cock. Each movement of his mouth filled me with a pleasure I had never experienced before, so much better than that of my own hand. He slid down further, and my eyes closed as the world tipped, a throaty cry escaping my lips. And then his hand was cupping my balls, stroking and squeezing them, alternating between pleasure and not quite pain that sent the room spinning like we were in a whirlpool.

I knew I wasn't going to last long as his mouth kept up the steady pace, my hands gripping the arms of the chair by my spread knees, my hips writhing against the velvet seat. I tried to choke out a warning, but Ambrose's mouth just worked harder at me, and the words lodged in my throat along with my breath. My hips pushed up eagerly towards his mouth once, twice, and then I spilled into his mouth, in the first release of my life not caused by my own touch. His mouth stayed on me, his tongue teasing and stroking the slit and head of my cock, draining every drop of my seed from it as the overly sensitive skin made me squirm and whimper. And then he pulled back with a wet sound, and I forced my eyes open through heavy lids to meet his. He wiped his lips that were red from his ministrations as his dark eyes grinned at me. My chest heaved under my shirt, my thighs quivering where the chair held them spread open. His smile was as intoxicating as the ship's rum and made my stomach flip inside of me as my cock gave another little twitch.

Ambrose leaned over me, his tongue pushing past my teeth to tangle with mine, and I could taste myself. My hands unclenched from the chair arms to slide up around his neck, fingers curling into his hair as I quivered under him, my tongue wrestling with his own, less confident but no less eager.

Ambrose finally pulled back to gaze at me, still so close that I could almost feel the brush of his stubble on my face. "That's a good lad," he purred, giving my cheek a tender kiss.

I blushed red and averted my eyes shyly as my fingers tangled further into his dark hair. "That was incredible."

Ambrose laughed at that. "I'm glad to hear it. It would feel even more incredible with my cock in your ass."

His words sent heat down my chest into my groin and my lower back, making me squirm on the chair as my softening dick seemed to find renewal in his words. Ambrose flashed me a brilliant smile. "Seems like you might agree."

My smile was shyer than I meant it to be, but I slowly nodded. "I... I think I would like that."

Ambrose's eyes twinkled, and he gently unwrapped my legs from the arms of the chair. "Stand up."

I wasn't sure if my legs would listen to me, but I carefully got to my feet, my shirt once again falling over me in a way that made me feel more like a child than a man. Ambrose gave me another kiss, harder and rougher this time, pulling me against his bare chest. I nuzzled my nose into it, inhaling the sea air smell. He laughed softly and stroked my hair before catching my chin in his hand. "Turn around."

I did as he asked, and he suddenly grasped my hands and pulled them down so I was bent over the chair at the waist, holding the arms of the chair for support. I shivered, adjusting my feet to find a good balance. My shirt hung down and open like a sail, and Ambrose pushed it up over my ass. Cool air met my skin, and I shivered. Ambrose leaned down to press a kiss to the small of my back, making me squirm. "Spread your legs for me, Jamie," he prompted, and, despite the slightly embarrassed blush that flooded my whole body, I moved my legs further apart as he asked.

His hands slid down, each one grasping a globe of flesh, and he squeezed it firmly. I gasped, leaning back into his hands. "Captain..."

"Miles," he corrected again.

"Miles," I said softly, glancing over my shoulder at him. He gave me a rakish grin, giving my cheeks another squeeze before he pulled them suddenly apart, and cold air met my virgin pucker of flesh. I squirmed, holding tighter to the arms of the chair, before I felt the press of his lips against the spot. I started to protest, but the sound became only a squeak when his tongue dipped out and stroked over the tight ring of muscle, causing it to clench even tighter.

Ambrose laughed, and I felt the brush of his stubble between my ass cheeks before he let go of one of them, and suddenly two fingers were at my lips. "Suck," he ordered. My mouth obediently opened, and the two fingers plunged inside. I gasped, trying to find a way to close my lips around them, then let out a rather embarrassing whine as his tongue brushed over my hole again. My own tongue darted over his fingertips, and he curled them a little. My mouth watered, and I tried to suck on them, jerking a little as his tongue brushed back and forth across my entrance, tickling and teasing and sending little jolts through me that felt so good I forgot to breathe. I moaned around his fingers and sucked on them as best I could, making little mewling sounds in my throat as he laved over me. I wanted to imitate his earlier movements on my cock on the fingers in my mouth, to give him a little pleasure, but I was so distracted by his tongue delving around my hole that I couldn't focus on much more than not drooling. Then his tongue breached my entrance, and I almost lost my balance with my arms, letting out a moan around his fingers that sounded whorish even to my ears. He laughed, and I felt the rumble in my tight passage as his tongue slid in further, then out, then back in again, lapping at me as his fingers sank deeper into my mouth, so deep it nearly brought tears to my eyes.

I don't know how long the movements of his tongue lasted. It might have been minutes, it might have been hours; I couldn't tell as my cock hardened and strained, my hips pushing back toward him even as his fingers began to thrust in and out of my mouth with abandon, and I was unable to do anything except let him. He suddenly pulled away from my ass, my hole quivering at the loss of his warmth, and I let out a whimper. He chuckled softly, giving me another squeeze. "So eager, lad. Don't worry, I'll be in you soon enough."

His words flooded my veins with heat, and I moaned louder before his fingers pulled out of my mouth, a long, sticky trail of saliva following them. I risked letting go of one of the chair arms to swipe at my mouth with my sleeve, then grabbed it again as the fingers were suddenly at my hole, the first one pushing inside and sliding deeper than I expected. The burn made me wince, but after my passage clenched around the digit and then relaxed, the finger began to pull out and push back in, and each thrust was easier than the last. I moaned softly, shifting to spread my legs even wider, and then cried out as his other finger slid inside of me too. I gripped the chair arms tighter, trying hard not to clench or pull away from him.

"Good lad," he soothed, his fingers starting to work in and out of my tight passage. I whimpered softly, biting my lower lip. His fingers spread me wide, and I gasped, hips bucking a little. My cock strained where it was, so hard it rested against my stomach even bent over as I was. And then his tongue was down by his fingers, licking over my hole, sliding inside me a few times before being replaced by his fingers again. I moaned breathlessly, feeling almost feverish under him.

"Stay there," he purred against the small of my back, and I obediently held tight to the chair arms, staying bent over as I was. And then Ambrose's fingers and mouth were gone, and he was up and moving away from me. I heard a breathless whimper escape my throat, and Ambrose chuckled. I craned my neck to catch sight of him. He was at his dressing table, where he selected a blue cut-glass bottle. He came back to me, pulling the stopper out, and the spiced, exotic smell of one of his oils met my nose. My heart gave a little hop in my chest, realizing that I would smell like him with that on my skin.

I felt his warmth press up against my ass from behind. I gasped, then whimpered softly as I felt the head of his cock nudge at my entrance, slicked with the oil. He felt impossibly large, and I fought the urge to pull away. "Shh," Ambrose murmured in my ear, one hand holding himself in position against me, the other wrapping around my waist to gently stroke my cock with his fingers. My hips bucked toward the touch, his own hips following mine, and then the head of his cock entered me. I cried out softly as the heavy heat pushed slowly and methodically inside, stretching me wider than I could have imagined.

"Good lad," Ambrose soothed in my ear again. "You can take it. Just relax." His fingers continued to move over my cock as he pushed further and further into me. I tried to relax as he suggested, though my body fought me most of the way until I felt his hips press up firmly against me from behind. "There now," he soothed, giving my cock another languid stroke. "There's a good lad."

He was still, his heat warm against my back as I gripped the chair arms, trembling a little as my body fought to adjust around him. His fingers caressed over the tip of my cock, made slick with a drop of seed he found there, and I moaned, my hips unconsciously rolling at the touch. Ambrose slid his thumb up, a bead of my desire still on it, pressing it to my lips. I obediently licked it off, shivering, then let out a cry as his hips pulled back and then pushed into me again. His thumb brushed my throat, as if to quell the noise. "Shh now," he said in my ear, his stubble grazing my skin as he bent over me. "It will pass." He held my waist with one arm, sliding his other hand down to play with my cock as he started to move inside of me.

I thought each thrust might split me apart, the next one deeper than the last. His hand stroked me in time with the movement of his hips. My arms trembled, and I couldn't hold myself up that way anymore. With a groan, I lowered my upper half so I could rest my arms on the seat of the chair, my forehead between them, as if I were bowing to some pagan god, which pushed my ass higher in the air. Ambrose grunted, pausing in his thrusts to roll his hips against me, and that felt so good. I moaned softly, and he did it again. "Your ass is to die for, Jamie," he groaned. The words radiated heat through my body, and I flushed with pleasure. And then he was back to thrusting, his movements a little easier now, bent at the angle I was. My shirt flopped back and forth like canvas in a storm, and I pressed my cheek into the soft, red velvet beneath me.

Ambrose shifted his angle slightly, and I suddenly saw stars in front of my vision as he thrust against something deep inside of me that made my whole body feel like it was as sensitive as the head of my cock. I cried out, my hips jerking back toward him, and he chuckled, his hips moving faster and finding that same spot with each successive thrust. This was how I wanted it to be, how I imagined it would be. No more pain, just pleasure and heat. My skin prickled as sweat broke out on my back and chest, my fingers digging into the velvet cushion as I let out a sound somewhere between a moan and a scream, my hips pushing back to meet his with every stroke.

His hand moved over my cock as he thrust, harder now. Somewhere in my mind I registered pain, but it was overwhelmed by the pleasure that rode through me, making my toes curl against the wood beneath our feet. I buried my mouth in the velvet cushion to muffle the sounds that tore from my lungs. Raw, animalistic sounds, hungry with need, full of heat and pleasure and the feeling of each stroke in tandem with the other. And then my pleasure peaked, my hips jerking as my passion released, some of it on the floor, some of it on the chair, and I almost collapsed. Ambrose's arm around my waist held me up as he continued to thrust, each one so overwhelming the world might have turned upside down and I would not know it. His hips pounded against mine, the slap of his pelvis hitting my ass and thighs from behind the only sound I could hear as my ears still buzzed with pleasure, my body shaking.

His own desire washed over him, and he gave a gusty shout, his hips jerking against mine and pressing so deep and hard inside of me that I thought he might fall into me entirely like a spirit. He slumped over my back, his warm, heavy weight pinning me to the chair seat as I struggled to breathe and focus on the world again. His breath tickled the hair on the back of my neck as he panted, then he pushed himself up, our bodies sticking slightly to each other with sweat.

He slowly pulled out of me, and I moaned loudly as his cock left my stretched and pulsing ass. My knees buckled, and I fell lightly to the floor in front of the chair, my heart racing, my shirt sticking to me in odd places and twisted out of shape. I rested my cheek against the chair seat, feeling like I might sleep for a week, or possibly swim the rest of the way to the island. My body trembled from the after-effects of my pleasure.

I was vaguely aware of Ambrose crossing to a wash basin and cleaning himself up before coming over to me with a wet cloth, which I took with a shaky hand. I did my best to wipe the sweat from my skin, and then dipped the cloth in between my legs. My hole pulsed as the coolness moved over it, making me wince a bit. I was going to be feeling that for a while. But I wouldn't have it any other way.

Ambrose took the cloth when I was done with it, then reached down and scooped me up in his arms like he had when he carried me to the chair, this time taking me to his bed in the corner, the elegant, four-poster thing with velvet curtains. He laid me down on the soft mattress and pulled a blanket over me. It was warm and heavy, stuffed with goose feathers, and I vaguely acknowledged in my sleepy state that I was glad Ambrose was a man who liked luxurious things. Then he was slipping into the bed next to me, even warmer than the blanket, and his arm went around me to hold me close. I nestled back into his embrace, and, within moments, I was asleep.

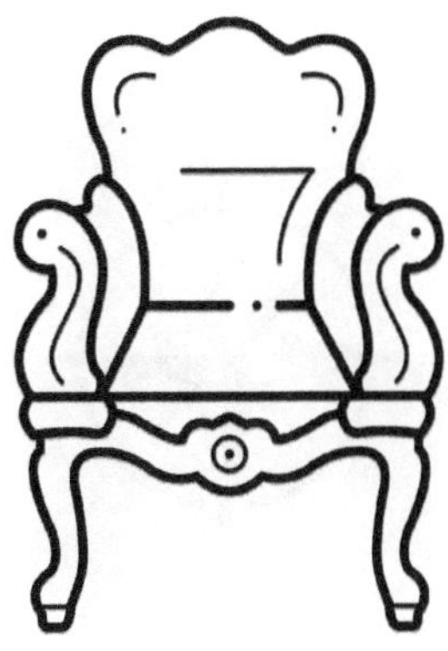

Chapter Eight

I awoke the next morning in Ambrose's arms, overly warm and sticky. The scent of his oil lingered on my skin, his scruff brushing over my shoulder where he lay next to me. He looked peaceful and content, and I stroked a few strands of his dark hair off his forehead. My heart fluttered under my ribs thinking of the night before, with our bodies entwined, fitting together so perfectly. I had not imagined that my first time with a man would be with someone as gorgeous and experienced as Ambrose, but now I could imagine no one else.

Ambrose blinked his eyes open, and he gave me a lazy smile. "Good morning."

I beamed back, leaning in to kiss him, and he tugged me close, his fingers tangling into my dark blond hair. I felt my prick give a jump, and while I was eager for a repeat of the previous night, both of us had duties to attend to on the ship, and I reluctantly pulled back. My body protested all movement when I sat up. The light was barely peeking through the windows of the captain's quarters, so I had at least not overslept my kitchen chores.

Ambrose watched me, a hint of that rakish smile on his face. I found myself suddenly unsure of what to do or say. It seemed rather presumptuous of me to assume that this would happen again, and I did not know what an appropriate topic of conversation might be at this moment. I pulled free from Ambrose and the blankets, getting to my feet, a bit unsteady, though whether from discomfort or the ship rolling, I could not be completely sure. I dressed carefully, feeling Ambrose watch me the whole time. Then he gave a lazy stretch, like an oversized cat. "Will you join me for dinner again tonight?" he asked suddenly, and I felt warmth flow over me like a bucket of hot water.

"I... I can," I said softly, meeting his eyes.

My stomach gave a sudden rather loud growl of protest, and he laughed. "I promise we will actually eat this time."

I beamed at him. Dinner with Captain Ambrose, just the two of us. "I would like that," I said.

"As would I," Ambrose replied before giving another stretch and sliding out of the bed.

I made myself as presentable as I could before giving Bosun a pat on the head and slipping out of the cabin. I made my way across the deck, the cool morning air freshening my skin until I reached the stairs to the galley.

Silas was already at work, boiling oats and water to make burgoo, and I moved to join him. It seemed like there was a frown on his gnarled face. He looked like he wanted to say something, but instead he was silent, and I was not about to offer him information he did not ask for or that was not his business to know. We worked in silence for a long time before he broke it with a soft grunt. "Is' no' my place to tell yeh what yeh can and canno' do, Jamie, bu' I care for yeh, lad, and I don' want to see yeh get hurt. Be careful."

Resentment roiled in my gut at his words, like he knew anything about Ambrose. "I will," I said, my words as bitter as tea leaves.

There was silence between us again for a long while before Silas spoke up again. "Jamie, 'n I ask yeh a question?"

I forced aside any lingering feelings of irritation and nodded.

Silas gazed back at me for a long moment before saying, "I'm jes a cook, makes no diff'rence tah me nohow, but I hear we's going after treasure."

This caused me to jump a little. I figured Ambrose knew, but beyond him, the squire, and Mister Kearns, I had thought that no one else was aware of the reason for our voyage. "Where did you hear that?" I asked, trying to keep my voice light, though I could hear the evasiveness in my own tone.

Silas's deep eyes stared at me, seeing something I was not sure of, and I shifted uncomfortably under the look. "It ain' my business, bu' if it's meant tah be a secret, I thought yeh'd wan' tah know that by now the secret's been told to the parrot, as it were."

The thought that every single crew member knew that we were sailing with a treasure map in our possession sent a jolt of fear into my stomach. The squire and Mister Kearns had impressed upon me the need for secrecy until such time as we reached the island and the true purpose of our venture was known. For while the hands aboard had been selected by Ambrose, they were still all strangers to us, and the betrayal of one could quickly become a mutiny if the situation became too heated. It didn't really matter where the information had come from, for there was no returning the rum to the bottle now that it had been spilled.

Silas's eyes were still upon me, and he said, with dead solemnity, "Where there's gold, there's also blood, Jamie. I jes wan' you tah be aware, lad."

Those words ran cold in my veins, for I had heard them before from George Conley. I swallowed, the motion getting stuck in my throat. "I'll be careful," I said softly.

Silas looked like he wanted to say something more, but he just shook his head and swiped some sweat from his brow. He returned to his work, and I returned to mine with a sobering dread that would not leave me.

My trepidation at the crew knowing the purpose of our mission stayed with me every day after that; I thought I could see greed on the face of every man who passed me. But Ambrose seemed to have ample control over the crew, despite many of them being older than he. He carried himself with a poise and authority that the men respected, even if they did often chuckle about his "fine and fancy" airs.

Our ranks numbered twenty, including every soul aboard, save for Bosun and any of the rodents that had found their way into our stores. The crew was a ragtag lot, ranging in age from only a few years older than me to wizened old Mister Thomas, who claimed to only be seventy-one but looked like he might have an extra hundred years on that from so much drink.

I came to learn much about the ways of seafaring men. Evenings were often spent playing dice or cards, and grog flowed like water amongst the sailors. Madsen and Vanders taught me to play cards, and Duncan taught me to cheat at them. The crew often told Duncan that the pockmarks that marred his face had come from the devil, one for each time he cheated at an honest game. He must have cheated much in his youth if that were true. Any time the devil was mentioned, Morgan would make the sign of the cross and then spit upon the ground. If there was a man said to believe in any sort of damnation, it was Morgan, and he always kept a well-thumbed Bible in his back pocket that he would pull out and read a random passage from any time it seemed convenient for him but not for those in his vicinity.

The youngest besides myself were Goode and Jacks, two men of early twenties, and they numbered amongst the lot Ambrose had brought aboard just before we set sail. They were not overly intelligent, but they were quick to lend a helping hand, and some of the more experienced crew members, like Miller and Reed, were eager to help them learn the tricks of the trade.

Then there was Franklin. He had been well brought up, had Franklin, before he came to sea. He was a man of quiet authority, much like Ambrose, and I laid that he would become the next first mate if Humbolt ever unexpectedly left this world. Franklin had wrapped around his finger a young man named Clark; I suspected them to be lovers, though I had never seen more than lingering moments of eye contact pass between them.

Thatch and Grant were the sort of grizzled men one might expect from a life of seafaring, boisterous and loud, among the first to start up a rousing shanty or swapping stories of ladies of generous reputation that they had found favor with at various ports.

The remaining member of the crew, the one who scared me the most, was Roderick, who near rivaled Silas for height and bulk, though was perhaps closer to Bosun in intelligence. His very presence was enough to fill any silence. In the first weeks of the voyage, it was he who made the crudest remarks to me. I found reasons to avoid being around him as much as I could, for the cold look in his eyes and his leering smile made me feel as though a fish were flopping inside of my guts.

One late afternoon when Silas had stepped out onto the deck to talk to some of the crew, Roderick found me in the galley and pressed me against the wall, offering me a silver coin if I got down on my knees and sucked his cock right there. I refused, to which Roderick grabbed me by the hair. I might have had rather a bad time of it if Silas had not returned right then and ordered Roderick out of his galley in a voice so thunderous and sharp that it might have broken my assailant like a smashed clay pot. Silas did not leave me alone in the galley anymore after that.

The squire was as kindly as ever, and he joked with the crew and made nice with all of them, but it was quite obvious that he was discomforted in their presence and often kept to himself in his quarters. The sea air and rocking of the ship was never something he got used to, and I am certain he was ready to finish our business and return home more so than anyone.

I learned that Mister Kearns was another old friend of the squire's, whose business was the import and export of goods, hence why he was familiar with the docks and those who sailed to and from them. He had known Ambrose for a handful of years, and their relationship was amicable. But Mister Kearns was of the suspicious and nosy sort, and he made it his business to boss everyone around as if he owned the ship. "A trifle more o' that man, and I shall explode," Silas told me one evening after Mister Kearns had criticized his organization of the galley, which he kept as clean as a new pin. Of that man, I have not much else to say, for he and I were not of such a mind that we spent much time talking.

Silas was unweariedly kind and always glad to see me. He had a way of talking to each and doing everybody some particular service. He kept things amiable amongst the crew, laughing at their jokes, joining in with some of his own. He did not speak of his time in the Navy with them, and I could not blame him, knowing how he was plagued with nightmares from his experiences.

I spent my days in the galley with Silas and my nights in the captain's quarters. After that first time with Ambrose, he invited me to join him for dinner every evening, and then we would spend the night together in his bed. I wondered if perhaps he would tire of me, or find another of the crew to amuse himself with, but his dedication to me and my pleasure did not waver. I, for my part, could not have been more delighted at my good fortune, for while I had not expected that our passions would cool immediately, I had not expected them to burn as brightly as they did.

For the most part, Ambrose kept his hands off me when the crew was around, though it was no secret that we shared one another's company and bed. The one time Roderick had made a comment about whether the captain was going to "share the wealth," Ambrose had shot him a look so venomous I was surprised the man did not drop dead where he stood, and no other mention was made of our relationship.

Some of the crew engaged with one another in a similar manner, though it seemed more out of sheer boredom than any sort of affection for the other party. Some were more discreet than others; more than once I turned a corner to find one of the sailors on their knees in front of another, or found them both pressed up against a wall. It was the way of the sea, and there was no fear of the laws of the land here.

While some of the sailors delighted in flaunting their prowess about, Ambrose reserved most displays of affection for his private quarters, where none could observe us other than Bosun. He wanted me all for himself, and

I was happy to oblige him. He took particular delight in sitting at his desk and working on writing or reading a book while I knelt under it and took his cock in my mouth, making it my sole mission to distract him as much as I could until he would toss his work aside to grab me by the hair and spill his passion over my lips. It took much practice before I could get his length all the way to the back of my throat, though neither of us minded the time that education took. After the sun sank into the blue waves on the horizon, I would curl in his arms in the darkness of his cabin, our legs entwined, the brush of his stubble against my cheek as soft as velvet.

I wondered to myself if this would last once we had completed our adventure. Ambrose did not speak of the future, and I did not ask, for it seemed rather foolhardy to make plans before our fortunes were made. But when I drifted off to sleep in his arms, the smell of his oils on my skin, his breath warm against my shoulder, I knew happiness as I had never known it before.

I am not going to relate the voyage in further detail, for our journey was quite uneventful in all other aspects. In this, I think all of us were quite content.

Chapter Nine

"Land ho!" came a shout from Duncan, above us in the crow's nest. I had been going over the last of our dried vegetables when I heard the call mid-morning, and I went sprinting up the galley stairs before Silas had even looked up from his work. I dashed to the railing's edge, squinting in the sunlight toward our destination. It took several long moments before I was able to see it, a dark smudge on the horizon, and my heart beat frantically in my chest like a trapped bird. It had been weeks since we had seen land, and I was more than ready to place my feet upon solid ground again.

Ambrose was suddenly behind me, his warmth enveloping me, and I leaned back into his embrace. "We made it," I said softly.

"Aye, we did," Ambrose said, giving me a gentle hug around the shoulders.

There was a great rush around us as the crew prepared to make berth. Mister Kearns and the squire were positively buzzing with excitement, the squire adjusting his hat over his wig, as he tended to do when he was unsure what he could do to help.

According to both the treasure map and the chart that Ambrose had on his desk, there was a southern bay area that was perfect to bring the ship into. I saw why as we approached the island from the easternly side, for that side of the island was a mass of rocks and towering cliffs, the waves crashing against the stones as if to smash them apart. There would be no landing there; even if we could, there was no way to climb the sheer faces with ease. I pictured the island in my mind and wondered if those great roaring waves and stony cliffs protected the treasure. Perhaps we were looking right at where it was buried without even knowing it.

Ambrose commanded the crew with the finest ease, having them prepare the jollyboats to take most of us to the island. Four crew members, including Silas, would stay aboard the MORAY to keep her safe and ready for our departure whenever our business on the island was completed. I stopped in my cabin, which I had barely been in for the last few weeks, to grab my compass, which I tucked into the pocket of my waistcoat, and then I headed down to the galley to say my goodbyes to Silas.

Silas had given me instructions on what sorts of food to look for on the island to replenish our stores, and there were casks set aside to collect fresh water for the return as well. If we found the treasure, we could also stop in one of the ports nearby and pick up additional supplies if the island ended up being less habitable than expected. I asked him if he wanted to come along to the island with us, but he said Ambrose had given him specific instructions to stay on board the ship. I wondered about that, as Silas seemed to know a lot about plants and wilderness survival, but I thought perhaps Ambrose was concerned that Silas with his single leg might slow us down, though he was quite proficient at getting around just fine.

He pulled me into a hug against his burly chest, and I returned it. "Jamie," he said softly, "Yeh be careful, yeh hear? Watch yerh back, an' look ou' fer yehrself."

He said this with such solemnity that for a moment I forgot to breathe. I nodded slowly. "I will. And I'll be back soon."

He gave me another hug and ruffled my hair, and then I was heading up the stairs into the bright sunlight again.

The ship weighed anchor in the bay, and then the jollyboats were dropped, four in all, with most of the crew, including the squire, Mister Kearns, and myself. Mister Kearns rode in one, Ambrose in another like a mighty general, with Bosun perched upon his shoulder, and the squire and myself in one of the remaining ones. The water buffeted our crafts about, but the crew pulled the oars doggedly along, maintaining control over the waves, until the boats scraped the sandy beach and came to a jarring halt.

I got out of the boat with hesitant steps, for it had been a long while since I had been on land, and the ground being solid beneath me suddenly felt foreign. I helped the squire out of the boat, and I could tell that he was feeling the solidness worse than I was as he dipped a little, sweating under his wig and hat and jacket.

Ambrose stepped onto the land like he owned it, waving his hand toward a raised area from the beach, just ahead of the tree line. "We will build the encampment there," he said, his voice carrying to the lot of sailors. "Unload the boats."

The jollyboats were hauled up onto shore, and their contents were emptied upon the sand and carried to the clearing Ambrose had indicated. We had brought food and water, casks of rum, tools for digging, spare sails for tents, blankets, and other assorted pieces from the ship. The squire puffed along beside me, doing his best in his advanced years to help out.

Ambrose pointed to two of the sailors and Mister Kearns. "Here, now, Franklin, Thatch, and Kearns, you three go and find us some firewood, we'll be needing a warm fire come nightfall."

"Anything else you be needin', Cap'n?" Thatch asked, picking up one of the machetes from the contents of the boats.

"Shiver my timbers, Thatch, use your damn head," Ambrose said with a roll of his eyes. "Do I have to tell you to do everything?"

Bosun let out a screech on his shoulder. "Shiver me timbers, rawk!"

Thatch bowed his head. "I got it, Cap'n." He turned, and he, Franklin, and Mister Kearns disappeared into the trees, Kearns taking the lead, as he was wont to do.

The squire was red-faced under his wig, and I grabbed a skin of water and pointed to a large piece of driftwood down the beach where we would be out of the way of the men working. "You need to sit down, Squire," I told him gently but firmly, for he was a proud man who did not like to admit he needed help.

"If it will not inconvenience the crew," he said with an apologetic smile at Ambrose.

Ambrose waved his hand absently, too busy with directing his men to their tasks to give us much notice. I offered the squire my arm, and we walked the short distance down the beach to sit on the wood. I gave him the waterskin, and he took it gratefully, taking a long swig before handing it to me. He stared out at the rolling blue waves, a small smile on his lips. "We made it, Jamie, by God, we made it!" he declared.

I nodded, and the squire took off his hat and wig to wipe at his forehead with his handkerchief. "I am very sorry, my boy, that I dragged you into this whole mess for my own inadequacies. You should not have had to endure a trip such as this."

I smiled and shrugged my shoulders. "I don't blame you in the least, sir. I am glad to be here to help you. And once we have the treasure, we will settle your debts and make things right again."

The squire nodded at that. "Indeed. And you shall have your share, Jamie. And... I will understand if you will want to take your leave of me once it is done."

The idea of having money of my own to do as I pleased had been an incorporeal dream for so long until now that I was unsure what I might do with more than a few shillings in my pocket. That is, if we found the treasure. I could only hope that no one else had before us, and that the map was genuine. For if it was not, the squire would be quite lost, and I had no idea what either of us would do.

The squire surprised me further by giving my shoulder a squeeze. "Would you perhaps go on to serve under Captain Ambrose?"

My face reddened, not sure what the squire was implying. He had not ever commented on my relationship with Ambrose beyond basic pleasantries. But the older man just smiled softly. "If you are happy with him, I would not want you to hold back on account of me."

I flushed deeper, ducking my head a little, giving the squire a grateful smile. "I... don't know yet," I said honestly. "Let's find the treasure first before any decisions are made about the future."

"Quite right you are, my boy," the squire said, giving his knee a jovial slap. He reached into his jacket and drew out the oilskin-covered map, handing it to me. "Will you hold onto this until we are settled? I shall try to help out the crew as best I can with this creaky back, but should not wear my jacket while I do. This poor old coat has seen enough wear in its day. That shall be one of the first things I purchase for myself, a new wardrobe. My old Maggie would have been pleased with that."

I tucked the packet firmly inside my shirt, the slick outside of it cool against my sweat-dampened skin, as the squire placed his wig back on his head and fanned himself briefly with his hat before putting that on as well. He took another sip of the water before sticking it into the pocket of his jacket and rising to his feet. "Not as spry as I was in my younger days," he said with a chuckle. "Enjoy your youth while it lasts, Jamie, my boy, tally-ho!"

"I will, sir," I said with a laugh, offering him my arm again, which he took for the walk back through the sand to where the crew had started to erect some poles into the ground.

"Shiver me timbers," came a squawk from nearby, and I spotted Bosun perched on one of the nearby crates, cocking his blue and yellow head to look at me as we approached. "Shiver me timbers."

I reached out my hand toward Bosun for him to give my fingers an affectionate nibble as the squire let go of my arm and wandered a few paces ahead over to Ambrose, the two striking up a conversation.

The next moment seemed to happen as if I were seeing it from the bottom of a deep well. Duncan suddenly appeared behind the squire, and quicker than my eyes could track, there was a flash of silver across his throat, followed by a gush of red. The squire's eyes bulged for a moment, like he was not sure what happened, and they turned to me in confusion. He opened his mouth to say something, but another rush of red flowed over his lips and down the front of his shirt, turning the faded white to a shocking crimson in moments. He dropped to his knees, wavered, and fell to the side, convulsing as his body fought alternately for air and blood, and I could do nothing but stare at him until he went still, slumped on the ground as blood soaked into the sand beneath him.

And then my eyes turned up to Ambrose, who stood, unmoving, near the squire's prostrate form, watching him slump with impassive eyes. I waited for him to yell, to draw his sword or his pistol, to do anything at all as Duncan stood only steps away, the knife still in his hand. I heard my heart rushing in my ears, louder than the nearby crash of waves. Was I about to join the squire on the sand in a puddle of my own blood? Was Ambrose about to fall to the hands of a mutiny? I opened my mouth, sure that I was about to scream for lack of anything more helpful to do, when Ambrose's dark eyes met mine, and the sound choked in my throat like an unchewed piece of meat.

The captain gazed at me for a moment, and I stared back, unable to make myself do anything more. I stood frozen to the ground as if I had grown roots there. I could not move, I could not speak, I am not even sure I breathed, for fear it might be my last. And then he smiled, that silver smile that I had grown so fond of. "My apologies you had to see that, lad," he said, as if he were apologizing for Duncan kicking a stray dog, not murdering a man in cold blood on a beach in bright sunlight.

And then came a great shout of laughter and jeers from the trees, and two of the sailors came through, dragging a third man by the arms as if he were nothing more than a grain sack. His head lolled, and I could see crimson painting his shirt as well. My stomach dropped inside of me as I recognized Mister Kearns, also dead.

Thatch and Franklin dragged Mister Kearns over and dropped him atop the squire's body in an unnatural tangle of limbs. I felt like I might be about to lose my stomach, my legs trembling, as several members of the crew turned to look at me, and I suddenly felt like a wild hare pinned by the gaze of bloodthirsty hounds.

"What about the pup, Cap'n?" Miller asked, and his leer sent dread into the marrow of my bones as the implication of the words settled upon me like lead. This was no mutiny, at least, not one against Ambrose.

"Leave him be," Ambrose said, his tone light, waving one of his hands with a casual flick of his wrist. "He is of no threat to us. Right, lad?"

I nodded numbly, for I knew not what else to do as I stared at the two dead men only steps from my feet. One of the other sailors, I thought it might have been Roderick but could not be sure, said, "Can we at leas' have some fun with 'im, Cap'n?" and I felt an icy chill in my spine.

"I said, leave him be," Ambrose said again, his voice suddenly much darker and rougher. "No one touches him without my say-so, or I'll see the color of his insides."

There was a grumble through several of the crew members, but a vicious look from Ambrose made it fall silent again, and I forced myself to breathe. Ambrose waved his hand at the bodies of the squire and Mister Kearns before he moved over to me, suddenly blocking out the sunlight. I had always felt protected and comfortable in that shadow, but now I realized how much taller and stronger he was than me, and I had nowhere to run, even if my legs had been listening to my brain.

"You... you killed them," I heard myself force out from between shaking lips. Ambrose's smile actually looked slightly apologetic, though not the least bit sorry.

"I had them killed," he agreed, though the semantics of it felt pointless right now.

"Why?" I shuddered, wanting to back away, but I still felt trapped in his monstrous shadow.

"Oh, Jamie. Do you really think that the squire was intending to share the treasure with the likes of us?"

I realized that I had no idea what deal had been struck between Squire Harrington, Mister Kearns, and Captain Ambrose, but whatever it was, evidently it had not been enough for Ambrose. "He would have," I said desperately, as if that could bring the squire and his friend back to life. "He would have, you did not have to murder him!"

Ambrose's smile was cool and unflinching. "Such a tragedy," he said, his voice dour with false sorrow. "The voyage's contractors both dead from a terrible accident. The sea is such a dangerous place, after all. But no reason to not still seek the treasure now that we are here. We'll be needing your compass, though." He held out his palm, and I flinched as if he had struck me, though he had not laid a hand upon me.

"No," I said softly, feeling the lump in my pocket that suddenly felt like it weighed more than the MORAY's anchor. And I became very aware of the oilskin packet that held the precious map inside my shirt, that the squire had handed to me only minutes ago, not knowing that his death was to swiftly follow.

"I'll be taking it either way, Jamie," Ambrose said, his tone pleasant but firm.

"Cap'n," came a grunt from behind him where Vanders had been searching the squire and Mister Kearns' pockets and jackets. "The map ain' here."

Ambrose turned away from me to look at Vanders. "The squire had it in his jacket pocket."

"I jes looked, it ain' there," Vanders said, holding open the tattered, blood-stained jacket to reveal its inner pocket turned inside out. "Jes this wa'er pouch."

Perhaps my foolishness got the best of me, but I saw the moment and took it. I turned and ran with all of my strength for the dense jungle, already several steps inside the tree line before my absence was noticed. I ran fast and long, clutching the map to my chest under my shirt, the compass beating itself against my hip with each step. And then a great shout went up, and I knew that Ambrose had realized that my flight coincided with the departure of both the map and the compass. I forced my legs to go faster than they ever had in my life, as if the very devil were at my heels.

At first, I heard some crashing through the trees behind me, but I dodged left and right, hoping to discourage their pursuit. I do not know how long or how far I ran; it did not help that I had no idea where I was either. It was only when I was so exhausted that I nearly blacked out that I finally stopped. I had a stitch in my side, sweat pouring down my back, my hair clinging to my wet face. I collapsed against a large rock, willing my heart to slow its frantic drum beat. I bent double, coughing as I struggled to catch my breath. I listened but could not hear anyone or anything approaching through the brush.

I sat down on the rock and pulled the oilskin pouch from my shirt, undoing it to stare numbly at the map as I held it with shaking hands. My whole being felt too heavy as I stared at it. My mind was still racing, as if it had run ahead of my body. Squire Harrington and Mister Kearns were dead, by the crew that Ambrose commanded. The handsome dandy, with the silver smile that made my whole body feel like it was on fire, whose bed I had shared, whom I had let defile me in every possible way, was not the man I had met all those weeks ago in the tavern, or even the man who had stood behind me on the deck staring at the island only a short while ago. Perhaps that man had never existed, and I was only just now seeing through the veil he had draped about himself, darker than any shroud. I felt like I wanted to cry, but my heart was too numb to do anything except stare at the blasted map I held, the sole purpose for all of our grief.

I wondered if I could figure out where I was, but there were no obvious landmarks around me. I could see where we had landed ashore in the jollyboat, and where the crew had been building their makeshift camp. I had a general idea of which direction I had run, which would have put me somewhere toward the western side of the island. The treasure was closer to the northeastern side; our locations to it formed a haphazard triangle. At least I knew the pirates would not be able to find the treasure without the map. I had some manner of bargaining, though whether that would help me in the end, I knew not.

I wished I had thought to grab a waterskin, for I had no idea where water might be, or if it would be safe to drink if I did find any. I could already feel my throat aching from dryness. I remembered one of the survival tips Silas had conveyed on one of our long afternoons in the galley. *"If yeh can't find water right away, put a pebble under yehr tongue, it will keep yehr spit goin' and make i' easier tah swallow."* Rocks were plentiful in this dense foliage, and I found a small one, wiping it on my shirt before popping it into my mouth. It was warm from the sunlight, but still cooler than I was, and while it was not a solution, it provided me some relief.

I realized I was going to have to sleep out here tonight, a prospect that filled me with utmost dread, for I had never been much of an outdoors adventurer in my childhood. I had no idea what manner of beast might make its home on an island such as this; I could not even be sure that I could identify a creature if I saw it. But leaving myself exposed to the elements seemed less wise, so I studied the map further. There was a sort of mountainous rocky area further west, and I figured that was as good of an option as any for finding shelter. I pulled the compass from my pocket and held it until I was sure of my bearings before setting off toward where the sun had started its slow descent.

It had nearly disappeared behind the rocky area when I finally emerged from the jungle to find it. The shadows made it hard to tell what was rock and what was crevice, but after a bit of searching, I found an opening of a cave that was blessedly uninhabited by creatures, save for a few small crabs who scuttled away as I entered. It was not auspicious by any means, but it was cool and covered, and I was too tired from my grief and my escape to care about anything more than sleeping. I pulled the pebble from my mouth, stuck the oilskin packet under my head as a makeshift pillow, and I was soon asleep in darkness and dank.

Chapter Ten

The sun was only just rising when I awoke, stiff and cold in my makeshift shelter. Lying on the hard ground in a briny cave was a far cry from my last few weeks of waking up under silk sheets, but at least I was alive. I tucked the map away in my shirt again, checked the compass in my pocket, and then set about finding something to eat. I was shaky with hunger, and my throat felt dryer than the sand beneath my feet. I made my way into the jungle, finding some morning dewdrops on a few lower-to-the-ground plants, and I licked them up, praying that the plants were not poisonous. There were many trees with various unknown fruits hanging off of them, but my knowledge of such fare was untested. I found several birds pecking away at a citrus-type fruit that had fallen from a tree, and I figured if it was safe for the birds, it was likely to be safe for humans as well. So I plucked one of the lower-hanging ones and sliced it open with a jagged stone. The inside was sweet and a little sour. I made short work of its innards and then another one as well until my stomach no longer pinched with hunger. I was sure I could have eaten the whole tree-full of whatever these were, but I had to keep my wits about me.

And then I found myself quite at a loss of what to do. The squire and Mister Kearns were dead, killed by Captain Ambrose and his crew members on the beach. Was there anyone on the ship I could trust, or were they all under the sway of Captain Miles Ambrose? Had he enchanted all of them the same way he had enchanted me, with his rakish grin and poisonous words? Words that he had dripped into my ear night after night, words that I had absorbed like a sponge because he was handsome and made me feel special. My heart ached in my chest as I wondered if anything that had come out of Miles Ambrose's mouth had ever been true, or if the man was a construction of nothing more than lies and charm.

I could not trust anyone currently on the island with us, that much I knew. I remembered Ambrose mentioning that first day we had met him at the inn that he was looking for a few more hands, and I thought these last few men he brought on were the least likely to be under his power. But for the life of me, I was unsure if any of them could be trusted, save for one. My friend and kindly companion, Silas Cross.

As I considered my interactions with Silas during the weeks we had been in each other's company, it made sense in my head that he was not likely to have anything to do with Captain Ambrose's mutiny. He had come on late; he was an ex-privateer in the King's Navy; he had taken the lowly job of cook; and due to his scarred face and darker skin, many of the men thought him to be simple, which I thought laughable. Silas Cross was as clever a man as Ambrose, perhaps more so. I felt sure that amongst any of the crew, Silas Cross was the one man I could trust.

Reaching him, on the other hand, would be a challenge. He was still on the ship, as far as I was aware, and there was no way to steal one of the jollyboats by myself. I could attempt to swim from the beach to the ship, which was a terrifying prospect considering that I did not know how to swim, and the waves had buffeted even our proper crafts about. I was far more likely to be dashed upon the rocks than I was to make it safely to the MORAY. The other possibility was to hide in one of the jollyboats in the hope that they would return to the ship for supplies, but that could be hours or even days away, and there was no guarantee which jollyboat they would select. Once I was hidden in one, I would have no opportunity to change boats or deviate from my plan without risking exposure.

Even if I did reach the MORAY and Silas, I could not be sure that the remaining crew members aboard could all be trusted, and there was no way that Silas and I could bring the ship safely across the sea by ourselves. Dread gathered in my gut as I realized that there might not be a way off of this island that did not involve returning to Ambrose. The only bargaining chip I potentially had to save my own neck was the map and the compass. I could not let him have both, or my life would be as easily forfeit as the squire's.

I found a hollow tree and stuffed the map deep inside its rotting core. To be sure I could find it again, I scratched a deep gash into the bark at its base, and then I made small arrows with rocks, from several different angles, pointing the opposite direction of the tree so it was in the center of its own compass. Hopefully, if anyone were able to find my arrows, pointing them in the opposite direction would send them on a merry chase. The compass I kept in my pocket, for it would serve me in retrieving the map and finding my way back to the fort, and I was reluctant to part with it in any case.

I spent much of the day foraging for food and water, hiding in my cave during the hottest hours. I was nearly giddy with heat and lack of nourishment by the end of the first day, and the night was cold and lonesome and miserable.

The second morning after my flight from the pirates, I checked that the map was still securely hidden, and then I proceeded to forage again. I could not seek out the treasure on my own, for I had no means to dig it up even if I did find it, nor would gold mean anything to me without sufficient water and food. Several times throughout the day, I heard or saw glimpses of the pirates in the jungle, no doubt looking for me. But if any of them were aware of my presence, they did not betray it, and I returned to the cave for another night in my grief and loneliness.

The third day brought one of the pirates into my path as I was foraging. He approached me, waving a dirty handkerchief as a white flag of truce, as if afraid I might decide to shoot him where he stood, though I had no weapon. I held my hands out from my sides so he would keep his own weapons stowed.

"'Ey, Jamie," the man said, and I recognized Madsen. "I've come 'ere with a message from Cap'n Ambrose fer yeh."

"You can tell it to me from there," I said, and he paused a dozen feet or so from me. Madsen was not the largest of the crew, but he could still easily overpower me if he wanted to.

Madsen lowered the handkerchief and mopped his brow with it, a lighter line appearing where the cloth wiped away the grime. "Cap'n Ambrose says 'e wants ta make a trade with yeh," he said.

"What kind of trade?" I asked cautiously.

Madsen smiled, the space between his front teeth looking even more pronounced than usual. "'E's got Cross."

My stomach suddenly dropped inside of me, and I nearly crumpled. Madsen grinned his gap-toothed grin. "'E's givin' yeh til tomorrow mornin'. 'E says yeh can give 'im the map an' the compass, or 'e'll send Cross ta the great beyon'. Affer 'e takes off 'is other leg fer the trouble."

I started to shake. "If I give him the compass and the map, what then?"

"'E says once the treasure is aboard the ship, 'e'll let both you an' Cross go. 'E's willin' ta negotiate them terms with yeh. And," Madsen reached for his belt, holding up a skin of water that sloshed, and my parched tongue ached. "'E sens this ta yeh, as a jester o' good will."

I wanted to grab the waterskin, fairly certain that Ambrose would not try to poison me without having the map in his possession, but I was learning very quickly not to trust Captain Miles Ambrose. "You take a drink first," I said to Madsen.

He smirked. "Cap'n said you'd say tha'." He flipped open the cap of the skin, pouring a few drops onto the handkerchief in his hand, which stayed its dirty white, and then he lifted the skin to his mouth and took a big swallow, smacking his lips with obvious relish. I watched him carefully, and he wiped at his brow again with the damp cloth. When a minute had passed and nothing had happened, I held out my hand for the waterskin. Madsen tossed it, and I caught it with a heavy slosh in my hands. I am not ashamed to admit I tore the cap off and poured the water into my mouth almost enough to drown in it. The first few drops were the sweetest thing I had ever tasted in my life.

I slowed my drinking, knowing that to have the water come back up again would be a terrible waste, and the skin was only a third full when I stopped and hung it at my side. Madsen watched me with obvious amusement. The water seemed to have returned the thoughts to my brain. "Tell Captain Ambrose I will come tomorrow morning with the compass and the chart," I said slowly. "But if he harms Silas in any way before then, I swear on my life I will burn the map to ash."

Madsen nodded, giving me an exaggerated bow before he turned and disappeared into the trees, leaving me once again alone in the tropical wilderness.

I sat down to evaluate my options. I could not leave Silas in Ambrose's hands. But once I handed over the map and compass, what reason did he have to keep either of us alive? He could give his word, but I had learned the hard way that Captain Miles Ambrose was not someone whose word could be trusted. With no more than myself on my side, I was hopelessly outnumbered. I settled back against a tree with black despair in my heart.

And then it came to me, like a flash of lightning. For Ambrose to 'have Cross', he would have brought him to their fort. Perhaps if I slipped in during the night, when they were sure to be heavy with drink, I could free Silas, and we could make our way back to the MORAY where we might find help. It was not a great plan, but it was the best I had at the moment.

The compass was heavy in my pocket as I started toward the beach to find the pirate camp. It was not very difficult, for thirteen pirates, a captive, and a parrot were not a quiet bunch. I found their encampment, the area surrounded by a hastily constructed fence. I took up a place just inside the tree line, and I thankfully also found a tree laden with bananas, so I was able to fill my cramping belly. And then there was nothing I could do but wait until darkness fell.

They caroused far into the night, drinking more and more until most of them stumbled and slept where they fell. Ambrose himself did not join in the drinking, and this worried me, for his senses were as sharp as the edge of his blade. But long after the moon had risen, I could only hear snores from the assembly. One man, I thought it to be Thomas, stood guard with a torch by his side, but even he had imbibed enough that he was not entirely awake, and I circled around to the back of the enclosure with the lightest steps I could muster. I found a place where there was a gap between the fence posts, and I squeezed through it, grateful in that moment for my wiry nature. Silas and I would have to leave by the guarded entrance, but one lookout was much easier dealt with than a crew.

Sails had been erected with poles to create a sort of tent-like structure to protect the pirates from the elements. Silas had to be inside with them, as I saw nothing beyond a few men lying about in the throes of intoxication outside the canvas structure. I slipped into the tent and nearly trod upon a man who had taken up sleeping quarters against the edge. He merely snored louder, and I stood still in the dimness until my eyes had adjusted.

Makeshift hammocks and berths had been scattered around in a haphazard fashion. I was going to have to move like a maiden at a dance to get through them. I was starting to regret my choice to be here, until I caught sight of Silas. He was nearly all the way across the tent from me, lying on his side. His hands were bound behind him, and the rope was then secured to his single ankle, essentially hog-tying him in place. His back was to me, so I did not know if he slept or was awake, though I could see the rise and fall of his chest to know that he yet lived.

I cautiously picked my way through the sleepers, having to jump aside more than once as someone would toss about in their stupor. I had just begun to think that perhaps I would make it when a screech sounded above my head, a sound that might have turned my hair white. Bosun dove at me, and I found myself beating at his bright blue feathers as he flapped about my face, squawking to wake the dead.

I turned to flee and ran full into the arms of Captain Ambrose, who for his part closed upon and held me tight. "Ah, Jamie," he said as I kicked and struggled. The noise around me was suddenly deafening, and my eyes burned as several torches were lit, nearly the entire crew staggering to their feet like monsters risen from the grave. I screamed and thrashed, but Ambrose held me tight. "You are only wearing yourself down, lad."

I knew he was right. Even if I managed to break his hold, there was nowhere to run, as I now had a score of pirates between me and any sort of escape. I had been played the fool, and now Ambrose had me too. I stopped fighting, my limbs going limp in his embrace, and I chanced a glance at Silas. He had rolled to the other side so I could see his face now. He sported a black eye, and dried blood crusted his forehead from a wound there, a dirty handkerchief tied around his mouth as a gag, but he seemed alert and otherwise unharmed. How long that would last was anyone's guess.

Ambrose tied my hands behind me but left my feet unbound, for where would I possibly be able to run? Some of the crew went back to sleep, others stayed awake and began a spirited game of dice. Ambrose led me outside of the tent and over to a nearby pile of firewood, pushing me down to sit upon it, and he perched next to me, the vision of sincerity.

"Well now, Jamie. It seems we have found ourselves at a crossroads. You've put me in a rather difficult position, you have."

I glared at him but said nothing. Ambrose sighed. "I've always liked you, lad. You're the picture of my own self when I was younger."

"I am certain I am more honest than you have ever been," I forced out, and Ambrose let out a guffaw of laughter.

"There ain't no fortune in honesty, Mister Davis. I'm sure you will understand that one day soon. But now, let us have a discussion, man to man, as it were." He gave me a smile that reminded me much of my Uncle Ned when he would ask me a question and I would give the correct answer in return. "The way I see it, you have two choices. You can join my crew, seek out the treasure with us, and get a full share. Or you can die here, with no one to mourn your passing save for Mister Cross, who will presently suffer the same fate."

I shuddered at this. Ambrose wrapped an arm around my shoulders and pulled me closer against him. Despite the revulsion that turned my stomach rancid, I was oddly grateful for his warmth in the chill of the ocean's breeze. Suddenly, being in his embrace again was so familiar that my heart gave a quiver under my ribs, like a bird woken momentarily from slumber.

"Am I to answer, then?" I asked with a very tremulous voice.

"If you have your reply," Ambrose replied. "But take your bearings. You're free to answer no, but what would be the good of that? There really is only one path for you, my lad. I always wanted you to join and take your share. We're shipmates, aren't we, Jamie? And we could be so much more." Ambrose's thumb ran down my cheek. "Time goes so pleasant in your company, you see. And with the treasure, we'll be rich men."

A shudder went through me as Ambrose stroked my face. "You killed Squire Harrington and Mister Kearns. Why do you think I would help you?"

Ambrose's face visibly darkened even under the moonlight. "Now, look you here, Jamie Davis," he said in a steady whisper that was no more than audible, "you're within half a plank of death, and what's a long sight worse, of torture. If you refuse my offer now, well... I can't be responsible for what my crew decides to do with you. But if you are with me, you mark, I'll stand by you through thick and thin."

His words sent a tremor through my body. Without Ambrose's protection, I was as good as dead, and Silas would likely be as well. I swallowed, but Ambrose was not done. "I like you, lad, make no mistake about that. You know the life I live. I can give you luxury you've only ever dreamed of."

"What are you offering me, Captain?" I said cautiously, fairly certain I knew the answer but wanting to hear it aloud.

Ambrose smiled that smile that once had made my heart flutter but now made my skin crawl. "I think you know what I mean, Jamie," he said, giving my cheek another stroke. "I'd be proud to have you by my side."

"You want to keep me like a paid whore," I ventured, my tone gruffer than I meant it to be.

Ambrose threw back his head and laughed long and loud at that. "Smart as paint you are, lad. But come now, let's not be crass. Gentlemen of fortune together. A life of easy living, with no cares in the world, doing whatever we like. Does that not sound better than living forever in your master's debt? Or the few more days you would survive on this island, alone or in the hands of my crew?"

I wanted to rail against him and tear out his throat with my fingernails. He played with a stacked deck, and he knew where all the cards were, while I could only bungle my way through. Ambrose had said, only minutes ago, that there was no fortune in honesty. If I played his game, I could potentially come out the victor. I swallowed hard, then looked up into Ambrose's face, giving him the best cherubic-eyed stare I could. "Will you let Silas go free if I do?"

Ambrose gave me a poke in the ribs. "You try so hard to play innocent, lad. I ain't falling for your tricks. But I like you, make no mistake about that. Join with me, and, provided he doesn't look me cross between the eyes, I give my word that I won't harm him." He chuckled at his own little joke.

"Your word is hardly worth a biscuit, Captain," I said, glowering slightly.

"Now, Jamie, that's not fair," Ambrose said. "I never lied to you. Omitted the truth, aye, I'll admit to that, but I didn't lie. And I ain't lying to you now. I swear I'll not let harm come to him if you stay with me. I'll swear it on my mother, God rest her soul. I'd even swear it on a Bible if I had one."

I still had no trust in his words, for the man was no Christian, and I knew nothing of his mother but that she was dead and he was beyond her reproach. But I had very little else to bargain with, other than the map and compass. I could not agree to everything quickly without arousing his suspicion, but I could at least play along until I had a way to get Silas and myself out of this trap. If Ambrose knew my fear, he could exploit it further, and Silas's life could be forfeit. "One thing I'll say, and no more," I said slowly. "If you spare him, bygones are bygones. I will cooperate with you if you give your word, as a gentleman of fortune, that you will not harm Silas and will set him free without injury once the treasure has been found."

Ambrose placed a hand on his heart, as if he were swearing an oath to king and country. "It's a bargain," he said, solemn as the clouds that passed over the moon. "Give me the map and the compass, and come daybreak, we will make rich men of ourselves."

"The compass is in my pocket," I said, shifting a little but unable to reach for it with my hands tied behind me. "The map I have hidden, and it will remain so to ensure that you uphold your end of our agreement, Captain."

Ambrose's dark eyes glittered in the moonlight, but he nodded. "Aye, lad, you be no fool, and I admire that. I'll take that compass, and tomorrow we will fetch the map."

"Agreed," I said, for lack of anything more I could say. About the treasure, I cared not, but I cared whether Silas would live to see another day.

Ambrose rose to his feet and stretched, then slid his hand down the front of my shirt. His fingers brushed the waist of my trousers, and I was ashamed to feel my prick jump a little. Despite my revulsion of him, his touch entranced me with some sort of spell that I could not resist. I inhaled softly, trying to will myself to not revel in his touch. His hand drifted just below my navel before suddenly skirting to the side and ducking into my pocket to take the compass out. My hips gave a little jerk at the tease, and I swallowed hard. Ambrose checked the compass over, then tucked it securely into the pocket of his own breeches. "What say you, lad? Shall I take advantage of you not being able to use your hands?" His palm grazed down my hip lightly, and though my stomach twisted, I was unable to stop myself from leaning slightly toward him.

"No," I said, even as my cock threatened to betray me to him.

He gazed at me for a moment before removing his hand from my hip and stepping back with a nod. "I may be a pirate, Jamie, but I ain't no monster. One day you will want me again, but I will not force it from you. Come, let's get some sleep." And with that, he led me back to the tent where Silas lay watching us approach. I gave my friend a nod, at which he seemed to relax a little. I laid on my side, hands still useless behind me. Ambrose tucked a blanket around me, and I was grateful for the meager warmth. And then, on that cool, sandy beach under the flapping canvas tent, surrounded by all variety of villains, I slept.

Chapter Eleven

I was awoken from my restless sleep by a frantic shout. Jerking awake to a commotion toward the entrance of the tent, I twisted around so I could sit up, my hands still firmly tied. Dawn light was spilling in, and Miller was yelling, his tanned face as white as if his spirit had been plucked from him. At his feet, two of the sailors lay, their throats slit from ear to ear, leaving a gaping smile in their necks where there should not have been. Neither one had woken from his slumber. One was Thatch, the other Vanders.

There were shouts and screams and curses flying as others awoke to the same horror I did. Someone had killed those two men in the middle of the night, getting past the guard and not waking anyone inside the tent. My stomach filled with sour dread, and it took everything in me to not heave my guts out on the floor.

Captain Ambrose was up and over to the crowd, shoving the men aside to kneel by the corpses. He turned to the crew with fire in his dark eyes. "Who was to be keeping watch last night?" he demanded, looking around.

The men fidgeted before Ambrose's eyes landed on the scraggly-bearded older man with bleary, red eyes. "Thomas! What do you have to say for yourself, man, for these two poor dead souls?"

Thomas looked positively baffled, cowering a bit as Ambrose stood to his full height. "I ne'er saw nobo'y, Cap'n," he said, his words slurred, though whether from drink or from nerves, I could not say.

"Their blood is on your hands, Mister Thomas!" Ambrose cried in such a tone that those around him shrank back.

Thomas held up his hands. "I ain' seen no one aroun' the camp, sir, sure'n the good lord above I ain'!"

Ambrose quirked a brow, seeming to consider this for a moment, before, in a motion almost too fast for me to make out, he drew his pistol from his waist, cocked back the hammer, aimed, and fired it nearly point blank into Thomas's chest. The man stumbled and fell back, landing on the sand with a heavy thump that shook me to my very core. He was dead before he even hit the ground, and I supposed that to be a mercy on him as Ambrose swiveled around to the crew, daring them to make a move. No one did.

"The next man to be derelict of his duties will answer to a bullet," he said in his strong, unwavering voice. "Who saw anything last night? Speak up!"

The crew shuffled nervously, but no one spoke up. Ambrose wheeled around, each one cowering a bit under his icy gaze. When it landed on Duncan and stayed there, the pock-faced man shook like a tree in a storm.

"Could... could it have been an evil spirit?" Duncan asked in a voice that trembled like he did not want to give word to his thoughts.

"The ghost of Cap'n Locke?" said Humbolt next to him in a feeble voice.

Ambrose raised a brow as some of the crew gave hesitant nods or questioning looks to their fellows. Pirates were a superstitious lot, I had come to learn. "I've heard foolishness from the likes of you, Mister Duncan, but nothing so foolish as that. The murderer is someone that's flesh and blood, you may lay to that. And when I find him, I promise you he will fall to cold steel the same as any other." The pirates all nodded uneasily to one another, for none were about to argue with Ambrose.

The Captain straightened. "Mister Davis is going to bring us the map this morning. Franklin, with me. The rest of you, get the supplies prepared for tomorrow."

"An'... them?" Miller asked, nodding his head at the three fallen, bloodied corpses.

Ambrose waved his hand. "Send them to the sharks with the squire and Kearns." And with that, he dismissed the crew from his caring.

Franklin came to Ambrose's side, and Ambrose gave me a cool smile. "We are taking Mister Cross with us to retrieve the map."

I narrowed my eyes at him. "Two fully armed men against myself and Silas with his one leg?"

"I am not about to underestimate you again," Ambrose said with a grin, grabbing me by the back of the neck and steering me toward the tent flap. Bosun swooped over our heads and alighted upon Ambrose's shoulder, and I had never wanted to strangle an animal more than that parrot at that moment as he began to preen his feathers, heedless of the danger he had put me in. Franklin hauled Silas to his feet, undoing the rope that secured his ankle to his wrists but not giving him his crutch that was propped against the tent wall.

Once we were out of the fort and into the cover of trees, Ambrose undid the bindings around my wrists so I could stretch my aching shoulders. "I'm sure you're bright enough to realize that any funny business will get Mister Cross here in a heap of trouble."

"I won't go anywhere," I promised bitterly, glancing over at Silas, who was watching me silently. "Can you at least remove his gag?"

Ambrose gazed at me for a moment, then gave me a smile that was surprisingly kind. "Aye, I can do that," he said, turning to Franklin. "You heard the lad."

Franklin glowered, but he pulled the dirty rag from Silas's mouth, letting it drop around his neck instead. Silas licked his lips and nodded. "Much thanks, Captain, Mister Davis," he said politely.

Ambrose slid his arm around my shoulders, and I let him. The more I was willing to go along with him and act like we might one day be lovers again, hopefully the more he would be willing to make small concessions to me that would keep Silas safer.

After a time, we paused for a short rest and to drink some water. I took the pouch from Ambrose that he offered. "May I give some to Silas?"

Ambrose waved his hand airily. "As you wish."

I moved to Silas, giving him a warning look with my eyes to trust me, holding the water to his mouth. He eagerly drank several large gulps before pulling back. I took out my handkerchief from my pocket, wet it with a few drops of water, and used it to clean the blood and sand from Silas's face. "Are you doing all right?" I asked, keeping my tone light.

"Yes," Silas said. "Are yeh?"

I nodded. "Yes. I have made a deal with Captain Ambrose."

"Jamie, no," he said softly in his low rumble. "Wha'ever deal yeh made ain't worth it with tha' devil."

"It's all right," I reassured him with a hand on his shoulder. "You will be safe."

"I don' need yeh to protect me," Silas said, but his tone was kind.

I gave him a weak smile. "You're my friend, Silas. I will not let them hurt you. Please, trust me."

"I trust you, Jamie Davis. It's that bastard I don' trust."

Ambrose grinned at that as he held up a cracker for Bosun to nibble on, like he was pleased with the assessment. "That's awful gracious of you to say, Mister Cross."

Silas glowered at him. "For God's sake, 'e's just a boy, Ambrose."

Ambrose raised a brow. "He's a man like you or I, and he don't need you babying him."

Silas looked like he wanted to argue, but I gave him a shake of my head. "I can make my own decisions," I said, looking pointedly between the two of them, and both of them went astonishingly quiet. While I appreciated Silas's concern, I did not need him raising Ambrose's ire and potentially bringing repercussions upon himself.

We started off again; I led the way, with Ambrose by my side. Dandy that he normally was, his black coat was looking somewhat worse for the wear, and I felt a tiny bit of pleasure when his sleeve snagged on a bush and ripped slightly. I tried not to go too fast so as not to push Silas, but he kept our pace as sturdy as any other. We paused to eat some rations and drink more water, and the sun was high overhead when I found one of my stone arrow markings on the ground. "Almost there," I said to Ambrose.

Ambrose nodded and waved his hand at Franklin and Silas. "I'll take the lad from here, you two wait."

Suspicion rose in my stomach, but I left the two sailors and walked by Ambrose's side into the trees until they were lost from view. When he was sure they were out of earshot, Ambrose gave me a gentle side-squeeze. "Just the two of us again, eh, Jamie?"

I glowered slightly at him. Only a few days ago I would have relished the moment to be alone with him, but now it sent an unpleasant chill up my spine. "You said you wouldn't do anything I didn't want."

"And so I shan't," Ambrose agreed. "That fire in your eyes is so pretty, though."

I had a childish urge to shut them, but I instead squared my shoulders. "Do you think my heart could ever be yours after what you've done?"

Ambrose sighed softly and actually came to a stop. "I can't change what I've done, Jamie. Neither can you. We can only go forward."

"That doesn't change the fact that you killed the squire." My voice was bitter, even as I felt hot tears sting my eyes.

"I did," Ambrose said with another sigh. "I have to admit that was a miscalculation on my part. Because I never thought I'd care about you like I do. But the plan was already in place, and I was not about to let the squire have what's rightfully mine."

I blinked at that. "What do you mean?"

Ambrose's smile suddenly changed, looking both sad and delighted at the same time. "By the powers, Jamie, you really had no idea the whole time, did you, lad?"

I simply waited. Ambrose sighed and removed his hat to brush his dark hair off his sweaty forehead. "I suppose it matters not now. Captain Locke's treasure has always been mine, by right of birth and parentage."

"Parentage?" I asked softly.

Ambrose nodded and gave a sweeping bow with his arm and his head. "Captain Miles Ambrose Locke, at your pleasure."

My mouth dropped as the connections finally came together in my mind. "Charles Locke was your father."

"Aye," Ambrose said with a soft laugh in his throat. "Not much of a father. Rare that a pirate ever is, I would wager. But he knew about me, and would come by from time to time. When he buried the treasure, he sent the map off to me, though I was nothing but a lad myself at the time."

"Then how did George Conley come to possess it?" I asked.

"Conley was a bastard and a thief," Ambrose said smoothly. "Never amounted to anything more than what he could find at the bottom of a glass. But I knew him. He had been an old shipmate of my father's, came through the inn my mother owned a few times when my father would come ashore. He became one of her long-time lodgers after my father died. When he had no more money for ale, he stole it, along with most of the inn's valuables, and then the slippery scoundrel disappeared. It took me years to track him down while building up my reputation and fortune as a gentleman. But he still had the map in his possession when I did. He was never of a mind enough to go after it himself. Always was a coward and a drunk, with no more courage than a field mouse." Ambrose rubbed at his chin with his hand as he said this.

"He was on death's door when I finally found him, but then your squire friend had to get involved. And I realized that instead of risking my own livelihood in pursuit of the treasure, I could simply offer my services to Squire Harrington when he became desperate enough to hunt for the island himself."

"Was it you who smashed the antiquities shop?" I asked, narrowing my eyes at him.

Ambrose threw back his head and laughed. "Not personally. That was Duncan and Reed and Madsen. Under my orders, of course."

"And you sent the black spot to George."

"I did. I had to speed things up, he was taking his time to leave this earth. Always been a parasite and a coward. If they couldn't find the map, I knew you or the squire would have it. So I bided my time and waited. I found the map, and I found you. A full deck of treasures."

I gritted my teeth, my heart aching as I realized that the kindly old squire who had been so good to me had been manipulated into seeking out Ambrose's help by the pirate's own hand. "Miles Ambrose," I said, "you're a prodigious villain and imposter. I don't dare to assume you feel any guilt for what you have done. But may the deaths of all those men and the squire hang about your neck like millstones, and may the devil take whatever bit of a soul you may have in your black heart."

Ambrose chuckled softly. "You do not know what you do to me, Jamie Davis. Even cursing my name, I still want to take you into my arms."

My heart ached ferociously in my chest at his words. Despite his sins, some part of me still wanted Miles Ambrose, silver tongue and all. But whether or not his words rang true now, I could not say. The squire and Mister Kearns were dead at his command, and Silas was his prisoner. His betrayal still hurt like a knife to my gut.

"Now," Ambrose said, slapping his thighs as if brushing them off. "The map, if you would be so kind."

I searched around until I found the familiar tree with its gash. I reached inside, drawing out the oilskin packet, and Ambrose made a soft sound of appreciation in his throat. "Smart as paint, you are, Jamie, my lad." He held out his hand, but I held the packet firmly.

"It stays in my hands until you let Silas go."

Ambrose stared at me for a moment, then shrugged. "Suit yourself, lad, I have no objection. But if you run off again, you know Mister Cross will pay for your actions."

I was not concerned for myself at this point, but Silas was another matter. I nodded. "I give you my word."

"And your word does mean something," Ambrose said with a sincerity that I hoped was actually true. "Come, let's return to camp and prepare for tomorrow."

Chapter Twelve

The four of us returned to the fort where tools and supplies had been made ready. The sun was already on its downward descent, and heading out into the jungle so late would have been a fool's errand. So we settled in for the night, Silas and I making dinner for the crew, who were in general good spirits once again. By the fall of darkness, most of them were quite drunk. I curled up on a mound of empty sacks, my hands once again tied behind me. Bosun came and perched on my shoulder, leaning in to give my face a nuzzle, but I shrugged him off. He gave an indignant squawk and fluffed his feathers at me before waddling off to search for bugs.

Silas was tied nearby, just his hands this time. He had assured Ambrose he would not attempt to run while I was still under the pirates' control. The idea of Silas 'running' with his one leg sent hearty guffaws through the drunken group, and I admired Silas's ability to ignore their jibes. I curled up and fell into a troubled sleep.

The sun had not yet even crested the horizon to illuminate the inside of the tent when there was a dreadful shout. It was Humbolt yelling, a screech like an animal caught in a trap. He was standing by the entrance of the canvas where he had come in from the night watch, a lit torch in his hand illuminating a dark pool at his feet, as well as the corpses of Miller and Madsen, both sporting wide gashes in their throats, as Thatch and Vanders had the previous morning.

Ambrose shot to his feet like a ball from a cannon, his tanned features unnaturally pale as he stared at the corpses of Madsen and Miller. He rounded on the crew, a madness in his eyes that I had never seen before, and my heart might have stopped in my chest at the fire in them. I felt myself start to shake. Silas sat next to me, his hands still tied behind him too. He gazed reassuringly back at me, and I forced myself to take a deep breath so as to not convey my disbelief. I knew I was trembling, and he tipped his head a bit for me to move closer to him. I did so, his great warmth soothing in the presence of more unnatural death.

"No one go' pass me, Cap'n, I swear it!" Humbolt said, and I knew he was remembering what happened to Thomas. "I were awake all nigh', ne'er even had a droppa drink!"

Ambrose stared around at the crew, seemingly dumbfounded. Much more so than he had the previous day when the first two sailors had been found sliced open. He gazed about the tent, as if looking for something out of place, but he found nothing. With a growl, he delivered a savage kick to

Miller's lifeless leg. "Get these out of my sight. Now!" he barked. The crew hurried to obey; I did not doubt it was to get away from Ambrose in the event he decided to blame someone and pull his pistol.

Ambrose whirled back around to stare at myself and Silas. Silas sat unmoving as a mountain, but I forced myself to pull off of his shoulder. I felt that Ambrose seeing me so close to Silas might provoke his rage further. He came over, glancing at Silas for a long moment before turning to me and kneeling, brushing my hair from my forehead. "Are you all right, Jamie?"

I nodded numbly, sure my face was still pale in the dim morning light. "Yes. Who would do such a thing?"

Ambrose was silent before he rose to his feet again. "No one will hurt you, lad. Not while I'm here."

Once Ambrose had walked away, Silas turned to me. "I hate to admit it, Jamie, bu' he does care abou' yeh."

I sighed softly, closing my eyes. "I know…" It hurt to say. Despite everything he had done, Ambrose still felt something for me, something that I wanted to return. But at the price of so many lives lost, I could not do it.

With the corpses disposed of and supplies packed, we all set off on our excursion. Ambrose was at the front with me and the map, Bosun perched upon his shoulder, gabbling odds and ends of wordless screeches, giving the gold hoop in his ear an occasional nip. Silas was somewhere behind us in the midst of the crew, at least given his crutch for the trek. Ambrose had tied my wrists loosely together in front of me and held the end of it, and for all the world, I was led like a dancing bear.

What I had imagined would be a joyous moment for the crew was as somber as a funeral procession. The terror of the dead buccaneers had fallen on their spirits. I could not blame them, for my own chest ached with undefinable fear at what might be lurking in the jungle along our way, just waiting to pounce. My own imagination created beasts from shadows more terrifying than anything that likely lived on this island. I even wondered if the spirits of Squire Harrington and Mister Kearns had come back to wreak their vengeance upon the crew of the MORAY for their mutiny, though I suspected the same as Ambrose, that the culprit was one of flesh and blood. What manner of man inhabited this island that could pass through our camp as unseen as wind and claim lives of sleeping men without waking the rest from their slumber?

The principal mark on the map was a river that ran through the center of the island, nearly cutting it in two, with a distinct bend to it. The instructions stated north by northeast from the bend, and we found the bearing through the trees with my compass. Roderick and Reed were at the front, beating a path through the brush with their cutlasses until we came out of the denseness of the jungle onto an expanse of flatter land. In the distance loomed the mighty rock cliff faces we had seen on the eastern side of the island when we had approached it aboard the MORAY.

We continued in this direction for some paces until those in front let out a great shout. Ambrose pulled me along next to him, and we found stretched out in the dirt before us, an old skeleton, covered with ragged, tattered clothing. Most of the flesh was gone from its bones, its jaw opened in a nightmarish grin. The legs, right arm, and head were all pointed in a straight line, but the left arm stood straight out from its body like half a T, its empty eye sockets staring vacantly at the rocky cliffs.

"What sort of a way is that for bones to lie?" Duncan said in a tremulous voice.

Ambrose let out a guffaw of laughter. "Old Hawk points the way," he said, nudging one of the bones with his foot. He checked the compass. "Northwest, this way. We are on the right track. Come, boys." He nudged his head to the left, toward the upward hills that the ghastly specter indicated.

The gradual uphill path became a rocky cove as we climbed higher, the roar of the ocean coming from below us rather than in front of us now. I realized why this spot had appealed to Captain Locke, for it was inaccessible from the north-northeast with the cliff face behind it, and the stony passage was such that it was not easy to stumble upon. We paused to eat and drink before continuing along the rocky crags when we suddenly rounded a bend to see two yawning cavern mouths in front of us.

"Which way?" Clark asked, and Ambrose glanced over at me.

"What say you, lad?"

I thought this might be a test, though of what I was unsure. I took the compass Ambrose held out to me, shifting this way and that until I was able to make sense of where we were. "The left, to the north," I said, and Ambrose smiled brightly. It was obvious that he had reached the same conclusion.

Duncan and Clark went forward first with lanterns, the rest of us following cautiously behind. The cavern itself was not overly tall, but we could still stand straight and raise a pickaxe overhead without fear of bringing the top down on our heads. The walls dripped with warm moisture that caused the air to have a smell that reminded me of seaweed and barnacles. Ambrose studied the final instruction, penned in his father's hand. *Seek within, 162 paces.*

As we neared the paces indicated, the ground in front of us seemed to suddenly drop off into shadow, and our party slowed. Ambrose moved carefully forward with his own torch, leaving me behind. He reached where the shadow fell and peered downward, then laughed brightly, the sound muffled by the damp stones. He gestured his crew forward, and there was much crowding and shoving. I kept close to the wall so as not to be dragged forward and eventually was able to make my way to see.

The drop from the edge was only about half a meter, though it was shaped similar to a bowl, all around the entire cavern. The inside of the rocky crater was filled with sand that seemed to have settled in several places. In one spot, something poked out of the sand, barely visible but for its dark shadow. My heart skipped a beat when I realized it was the iron-wrapped corner of a wooden chest.

There was a fantastic whoop, and suddenly Reed had jumped down into the crater, stamping his feet and kicking sand around to try to uncover whatever lay beneath it. Ambrose held up his hand, motioning to the assortment of digging tools with us. "Let's not be foolish about this now, boys. We have a lot of work to do."

The pirates set to work, tossing sand from the crater. The earth from the top was mostly dry and crumbly, but it grew moist and heavy the further they dug. Silas and I were tasked with bringing water to the crew. The thrill of riches seemed to have tripled their strength, for there was no bickering or complaints, save for when one pirate would get a face full of sand from an overly enthusiastic counterpart.

It felt like days, though I suspected it had only been a few hours at most, when the chests were uncovered. Though encrusted in filth from their burial, they were in surprisingly good order. One crate had a corner that had rotted away, and something spilled from its depths that I could not see in the cave's dimness, until one of the pirates held aloft a shiny, gold doubloon with a crow of triumph.

There were four chests in all, uniform in shape and size, the initials C.L. carved into the lid of each one. They were all closed with large, iron padlocks that still held fast despite the dampness and dirt that had entombed them for all these years.

Morgan raised his pickaxe to swing at the lock, but Ambrose held up a hand again. "Wait. Let's get them out of there before we start busting them."

There was a bit of grumbling, and I hardly could blame them, for my own curiosity was piqued, and I longed to see what was inside of this pirate's stash, but Ambrose was right that intact chests would be easier to move than broken ones and scattered trinkets.

The men attached ropes to the crates, and after many attempts, the four chests were pulled from their grave and to the open mouth of the cavern. The sun was already sinking, and Ambrose declared we would stay here for the night, for returning to the bay would be slower with the precious cargo, and none of us were eager to be in the deep of the tropical jungle in darkness. An area was cleared for a fire, and then, as Silas prepared a hasty meal from the supplies we had brought, the first of the chests was split open with a mighty swing of a shovel by Ambrose himself. The lid was thrown back with an ominous creak.

Inside the large box were burlap sacks of various shapes and sizes, but the first one dumped out upon the grass revealed a stock of silver ingots that glinted in the firelight. The next bag held a scattering of jewelry that looked as if it may have been crafted for the Queen herself. I was aghast at what we found in these chests. I knew Charles Locke had been a successful pirate of great renown, but I was unprepared for the sheer amount of decadence that spilled from the unassuming bags.

Jewels, coins of every denomination, strings of pearls, golden chains, figurines encrusted with precious stones, expensive silks that even outshone the ones in Ambrose's quarters. Most of the coins and statues were unfamiliar to me, and they obviously had not all come from the same location either. There were different levels of craftsmanship, design, and imagery, and I found myself studying a bas-relief that seemed to be made of ivory and had some of the most intricate carvings I had ever seen in my life hewn into it. I felt a sudden ache in my chest as I realized that Squire Harrington would have known the origin of this piece, and hot tears stung my eyes as grief settled over me once again. I refused to let the tears fall, for the pirates would have no pity for me, and I would not give them the satisfaction of my pain.

Just this single chest that was opened would have made each of us men of means. I could hardly imagine that there would be more in the other chests. A second one was broken into before the sun sank too low to see further, and it contained wealth much the same as the first. There was much celebration, with rum flowing like a river into the crew. Through it all, Ambrose sat near the chests, drinking no more than a single glass the entire night. At one point, Silas moved over to him to say something in his ear. Bosun fluttered over to me, perching upon my shoulder, nibbling at his toes with his long beak while Ambrose and Silas engaged in soft conversation that I could not hear. A few of the crew gave me a glass of grog to drink and spun me in playful circles while they sang a bawdy tune. Only when Roderick grabbed my ass and pulled me against him did Ambrose move, snarling at Roderick to take his hands off of me or he would be gutted like a fish, and the man released me with a leer and an apologetic bow to Ambrose, though none to me.

When the carousing died, the crew made their berths for the night, and I found myself curled close to Ambrose in the light of the dying fire. I hated myself for doing it, but his presence amongst the shadows and demons was more reassuring than sitting alone. He stroked his fingers absently through my hair, and I fell asleep against his chest that night in the dying firelight of the treasure island.

Chapter Thirteen

I awoke with Ambrose's black coat wrapped around me. The crew was in good spirits and the same number as yesterday. No mysterious attacker had come in the night to reduce our ranks. Indeed, that whole bloody affair seemed to have been forgotten as the pirates gathered the makeshift camp together, and we prepared to set out for our beach encampment again. Our supplies were substantially lighter with fewer rations to carry, and some shovels and pickaxes had been abandoned as well. The chests were heavy, much heavier than a man, so some harnesses were fashioned for the crew to be able to drag the chests along. Silas and I carried the supplies, and even Ambrose "got his fancy hands dirty," as the crew joked, by helping to pull the crates. Bosun sat on one of them, flapping his wings and clucking his tongue at the sailors, screeching out a beakful of foul words whenever he was jostled.

Going downhill was much easier than I imagined it must have been going uphill with these things when Locke buried the treasure years ago.

We followed our path back to the river bend, since the way had already been cleared, taking a break to eat the remainder of our food, and from there it was only a short trek to the beach and the canvas fort.

Ambrose directed the chests to be placed into the jollyboats. It was getting too late in the day to take them back to the MORAY tonight, but we could pack up tomorrow and potentially set sail for home. That thought made knots twist in my stomach, for I would be going home without the squire, to an unknown future that might or might not involve Captain Miles Ambrose.

Once the boats were loaded, the crew took the opportunity to splash in the sea water, and even Ambrose, Silas, and I joined in, for all of us were hot and grimy from the multiple days trekking through the jungle and hauling our treasures. Silas cooked an excellent dinner from the provisions at the campsite, the rum flowed again, cards and dice were thrown, and all seemed in as merry a mood as rich men could be. Tomorrow would be busy with preparing to set sail for home, and everyone was quite exhausted from the past few days' labors. The sun had barely set when we retired to the tent for the night.

It was nearly pitch black inside the tent, the barest scrap of moonlight illuminating the area, when I awoke with a start, unsure what had roused me. I sat up blearily, wanting to rub my eyes, but my hands were once again tied. I looked around, feeling that there was something amiss, though I couldn't figure out what it was.

Until my eyes landed on a hunched figure, silhouetted by the light of the tent flap, crouched low to the ground like a monstrous beast, creeping along the ground, moving deftly between sleeping forms until it stopped by the first mate. For a moment I was unsure what I was looking at, but then the figure's head lifted, and, to my shock, I saw that it was Silas, unbound. I must have gasped, for he looked up at me, and there was a hardness in his eyes that I had never seen before.

His eyes met mine, and Silas pressed his finger to his scarred lips in a silencing gesture. I clenched my lips firmly as I stared, not even daring to breathe. As deftly as any street thief, Silas plucked the knife from Humbolt's belt and sliced it as neatly as a surgeon across the man's bony throat. At the same time, his large hand came up to cover the man's nose and mouth, so the few jerks and sounds he made as he awoke and thrashed in his own blood were muffled, no louder than the snores of the men next to him. I felt the world spin, and I closed my eyes to keep myself from retching.

Once Humbolt had stopped twitching, his cadaverous body having gone even more corpse-like than before, Silas released the man's face, carefully wiped the blade on the man's sleeve, and returned the knife to Humbolt's belt. He wiped his own hands on the sleeve as well, smearing the blood so it was no longer recognizable. He made the sign of the cross over Humbolt's form before he began to creep back over toward me. I sat, transfixed, as I watched him; he lifted most of his heft with his arms and pushed himself along with the ball of his one foot, like some sort of humanesque cobra. Despite moving over jungle terrain, he was almost completely silent, no more than a shadow crawling across the floor, the soft underbrush and sand settling back down to disguise the path he had taken to Humbolt's side. When he was back to me again, he picked up the piece of rope that had been securing his hands and wound it around his wrists behind his back before resuming his sleeping position. In less than two minutes, it was as if he had never moved at all.

My heart thundered in my chest so loud it was a wonder it did not wake the crew. I rolled to face him. "Silas," I whispered.

"Shh," he said softly, and I could barely see the glint of the moonlight off his teeth in the darkness that shielded him. "I ain' gon' hurt you, lad, I'm keepin' yeh safe. Hush now."

I obediently closed my mouth on the questions within them, almost wishing I had not known the answer to the island's mystery. I knew Silas had been in the Navy and had killed before, but knowing and seeing were two entirely different things. Watching my gentle giant of a friend end the life of a fellow man so suddenly, and then feel obvious remorse over it when he blessed the man, brought so many confusing thoughts to my mind that I could not have given voice to them all if I had wanted to.

Was Silas any different than Duncan and Thatch and Ambrose? Was killing the pirates who would have no compunction about slitting anyone else's throat just as dastardly as murdering the squire and Mister Kearns? Or was it justice for the terrible things they had done? I could not decide, and my perilous thoughts kept me awake another hour or so, until one of the crew woke, staggering to his feet to go outside before tripping over the body of Humbolt and realizing with a great roar that the man was dead.

The camp was instantly awake, buzzing like a hive of angry bees as torches were lit to push away the darkness. Ambrose was mostly silent, watching his men. Mutiny, it was plain, hung over us like a thundercloud. It was only when Ambrose gave the order for Humbolt's body to be taken away that it all came to a head.

"It's a fine mess you've gotten us into," Duncan said, pointing his finger savagely at Ambrose. "A ghost hauntin' us, cuttin' us down like cattle. An' you do nothin'!"

"What would you have me do, Mister Duncan? Torture the lot of you until someone spills his secrets?" Ambrose asked, waving his hand airily.

"Oh, we see through you, Miles Ambrose; you want to play booty, that's what's wrong with you," Morgan snapped, casting a glance over at me. "You have your precious treasure and your molly boy, and hang the lot of us!"

Ambrose rose to his feet then, stepping between myself and Morgan's gaze. "Perhaps you can understand King George's English, sir. I'm captain here, by law and right. Not much worth to fight, the lot of you. You've neither sense nor memory, and I leave it to fancy where your mothers were that let you come to sea. I reckon tailors is more your trade."

"We'd all swing and sun-dry for your bungling!" Roderick snapped, and the resounding chorus of agreement shook me to my very bones. Silas sat beside me, silent as the grave, and I made no motion toward him, trying to not draw attention to us while their ire was focused upon Ambrose. What a moment it would be if he and I should have to fight for dear life against an entire crew of strong and active seamen!

I waited for Ambrose to draw a weapon or throw a fist, but he merely held up his hands. "If you have no faith in me, then I resign. Elect whom you please to be your captain now. I'm done with it."

This answer obviously surprised the pirates. I believe they had been expecting violence as much as I had. "What game you playing at, Ambrose?" Franklin asked.

"No game," Ambrose said with a shrug. "If you are unsatisfied with me as your captain, then I resign, by thunder! Make of that what you will, I'm sick to speak to you, and I need have no part of it." And this the more surprised me, for I thought he had never shown himself so cunning as he did then, keeping the mutineers together with one hand and grasping with the other after every means, possible and impossible, to make his peace and save his miserable life.

"I claim the right then to step outside for a council," Roderick said gruffly, and the others nodded. "Give us your hands."

"I understand how a deputation works," Ambrose said, and he held out his hands, wrists together. Clark came forward with a length of fabric that he tied around Ambrose's wrists, leaving the three of us bound as they turned and filed out.

I turned to Ambrose with wide eyes. "What's happening?"

"They're going to throw me off," Ambrose said calmly. "As I am the only one who might be able to put them off of it, I am not about to provoke them to violence."

My heart thundered, for if Ambrose was no longer captain, that did not bode well for any of the three of us.

"Be a good lad and go listen at the flap if you can," Ambrose said. "I'm curious as to how they may go about it."

"Shiver me timbers!" Bosun screeched from his perch on a nearby box.

I wasn't sure I wanted to know what 'it' was, but I obediently moved over to the tent entrance. I could not hear all of what was being said, but I listened faithfully. " ...the dandy that brought us all here and blundered us down to this, and that cub that I mean to have the ass of," Roderick was saying, grabbing lewdly at his crotch.

A couple of the crew laughed at that. "I say we cast him off right here," Reed said. "We have the treasure. If'n we off him and the cook, there's no one to put the finger to us 'cept the boy, and he ain't no concern."

"We can dispose of him a'fore we reach land," Duncan said.

"But we needs to do it proper-like now," said Franklin. "Rules o' the sea, and all."

There were a few mumbles that I could not make out, and my heart in my ears did not help the matter.

There was the sound of rustling, and then the rip of paper, several men letting out a hoot of laughter. "You don' soiled it now, Morgan," someone, maybe Clark, said. "'Ere come lightning from the sky to smite ya."

"I'll give the church double me tithe," Morgan said with a snicker. "The goo' Lord Almighty cares more 'bout that, I reckon."

"'Ere," said Reed, and I heard the scratch of something over the paper. "We need a time?"

"Nah," Roderick said. "No reason to give 'im time to think abou' it." And then footsteps began approaching the tent again.

I returned to my former position, for it seemed a head wise that they should not find me watching them. The group entered in a much more lively manner than they had exited. Once assembled, Morgan stepped forward and held out something to Ambrose. He took it between his bound hands, and I saw that it was a piece of paper with a circle filled in on it from one of the fire coals. My mind flitted to the similar paper George Conley had received from Ambrose that had signified the end of his miserable life.

"The black spot," Ambrose said, gazing down at the blackened paper. It had words printed on it, and I realized it was a page from the Bible that Morgan always carried. "Well, I suppose it's done then. Who amongst you shall be taking over as captain?" he asked pleasantly.

"Roderick," Duncan said, and I felt ice prickle in my heart as the burly man gave me a lascivious grin. I felt Silas stir just a bit at that.

Ambrose chuckled softly as he looked down at the paper, reading aloud. "'And said unto them, What will ye give me, and I will deliver him unto you? And they covenanted with him for thirty pieces of silver.' Well now. Was someone being poetic, or are you all really just a Judas lot?" Morgan suddenly looked very uncomfortable, shifting his feet uneasily. I suspected he had torn a page at random but might now be feeling the weight of the Almighty upon him for his irreverence.

Roderick snarled softly, then suddenly snatched me to my feet by the hair, and I could not stop a cry of pain as he hauled me up. Ambrose watched him with an impassive stare that chilled me to my core. Roderick pulled me back against him, and I flinched when I felt his cock press against my backside, his fingers bruisingly across my collarbone to hold me in place. "What say yeh, Ambrose? Yeh wanna meet yer maker before or after I have some fun wit'yer li'le bitch?"

I tried to pull away, but I was hopelessly pinned by Roderick's tree branch of an arm.

Ambrose gazed back at Roderick. "I told you not to touch him."

Roderick spat into Ambrose's face, and the former captain turned his head aside, reaching up to wipe the saliva away with the bindings that still held his wrists. "You ain' the one givin' orders 'ere now, Miles," he said. His other hand slid up to grasp the back of my neck and squeeze, making me wince. "Iyu'll let ya lissen while I make 'im scream. Then when I come back, I'll cut yehr beatin' heart from yehr chest and give it to 'im as a gift. Real poetic-like, don'cha think?"

Ambrose only gazed solemnly back at him. An icy chill went through me as Roderick shoved me by the back of the neck toward the tent's entrance. Raw, animalistic instinct kicked in, and I began to yell and thrash with all my might, even as he shoved me out into the island's cool night, the tent flap closing behind us. I screamed and kicked and bucked, as if possessed by the very devil, trying to pull my bound arms from his grasp, to run, to do anything, but Roderick gripped my neck like I was a newborn kitten, hauling me across the sand. I purposely slipped and sprawled, trying to roll away from him, but he caught me around the waist and picked me up under his arm like I were but a chunk of firewood. "Keep up tha' fightin', boy," he said, giving me a grin that showed his gruesome teeth. "I like when they scream."

I flailed and kicked, but my current position prevented me from effectively being able to do much. He carried me over to where the four large wooden chests of treasure had been loaded into the jollyboats in preparation for the morning's departure. He dropped me to my feet and then shoved me down face-first against one of the chest's lids. My feet slid in the soft sand as I struggled and fought with every bit of spite I had within me. My fists clenched and strained against the rope that held me, burning fire into my wrists. I heard the rustle of fabric, and my heart seized in dread as I realized he was undoing his trousers. It took him a moment to do so with only one hand, the other pressed to my shoulder to keep me in place against the dirt-encrusted wood of the chest, but then he grunted, and I felt him press against me from behind. He reached for the back of my breeches, and I closed my eyes, willing myself to not give him the satisfaction of tears. If he wanted a fight now, I would not give him the pleasure.

Something bowled into Roderick, knocking him sideways, and I rolled onto my back to see Bosun squawking and beating his wings about Roderick's head as the man tried to protect his face from the enraged bird's sharp beak and talons. His trousers were around his knees, and he tripped over them, falling into a heap in the sand. Bosun fluttered backward a few paces, just as a dark form materialized in the shadows. Bosun alighted upon it, and my heart skipped a painful beat in my chest as I recognized Ambrose coming from the darkness, unfettered and looking for all the world like a reaper of souls. He had a cutlass in his hand, and it gleamed silver under the moonlight, except where it was blackened with fresh, dripping blood.

Roderick backpedaled in fear, groping for his sword, but he had not thought to grab it when he had taken me outside, and his knife was tangled somewhere in the fabric around his ankles now. Ambrose stepped into the moonlight, the glow catching his shirtsleeves like a guardian angel. He glanced over at me, as if to be sure I was all right, before he strode over to Roderick, who was scrambling back across the ground, fighting his trousers and the slick sand to try to get to his feet and away. But Ambrose merely stepped up to him, gazing down at him like he was no more than an insect. He planted his booted foot between Roderick's legs, pinning him in place, making Roderick stiffen in pain. And then Ambrose's blade sank into Roderick's gut, so hard that it passed through his body almost to the hilt. Roderick let out a keening sound that made me shiver. Ambrose twisted the blade, eliciting a strangled howl from Roderick, and then jerked his arm up and back, taking the blade with it. I was thankful for the shadows of the night as Roderick's innards spilled over the sand, the man's wail of agony echoing off the trees.

Ambrose turned away from him and moved to me, pulling me upright before making short work of the rope that bound my wrists. And then Ambrose leaned in and pressed a light, chaste kiss to my forehead before wrapping his arm around me protectively, leading me away from the sniveling man on the ground. Roderick's groans faded behind us, and I could bring no pity to my heart for him.

Inside the tent were the remains of chaos. Besides Humbolt, there were three other men lying dead or dying upon the ground, but my heart leaped when I saw that the single remaining figure who was standing was none other than Silas. He had a dagger gripped in his hand, fire in his dark eyes. He was sporting a vicious cut across one arm, and his clothes were streaked with dirt, as if he had been rolling in it. From the state of the men by his foot, he probably had.

I dashed to Silas and threw my arms around him in a tight hug, and he caught me with an unexpected gasp of relief, dropping the dagger and pressing his three-fingered hand to the back of my head. "Jamie," he said in his rumbly voice against my ear. "Are yeh hurt, lad?"

"No," I said, pulling back to examine him as best I could. "Are you?"

"Jes' a scratch," he said, motioning to his arm. "It'll heal quick'n on the ship."

I nodded, then turned to Ambrose standing off to the side. I could see now in the lamplight that he also had blood splattered across his fine clothes, and I realized that he must have cut his way through the pirates to get outside to Roderick. I took a few steps toward him, holding out my hand to him. "Thank you, Captain," I said softly.

He took my hand with that smile I had grown to treasure, giving it a squeeze. "I am just glad you're safe," he said.

I nodded. "I am, thanks to you and Silas."

Silas moved up next to me, eyeing Ambrose closely. "A deal's a deal, Ambrose."

"Aye, it is," Ambrose said, and he held out the sword sideways to me so I could take it. Then he turned, clasping his hands behind his back. Silas tied Ambrose's hands tightly, and Ambrose said not a word, even held still until Silas was finished. Then he sat down on the pile of crates I had left him on only a few long minutes ago, Bosun nibbling affectionately at his ear.

Chapter Fourteen

In the morning light, the three of us dug a large grave to put the bodies of the fallen pirates in and marked it with a stone with their initials. Silas said it wouldn't be proper to not give them a Christian burial, seeing as how he and Ambrose were responsible for their deaths. I was sure he was thinking about the other dead men who had been tossed into the ocean like waste, but he did not say anything. The two pirates that had fled into the darkness of the jungle in the early hours, Clark and Franklin, did not reappear, and if the ferocity of Ambrose's dispatch of Roderick or the efficiency of Silas's dagger skills were any indication, they were much better off hiding in the trees.

We disassembled the tent and packed it into the longboats. The boats were tied together with a length of rope between each one, so we could take all four of them, piled with the chests of treasure, to the ship at once. Ambrose and I rowed us back to the MORAY while Silas steered. Though he made no motions against him, I was sure Silas was carefully watching every muscle of Ambrose's movement to ensure the man was not about to do something untoward. But Miles Ambrose was the model of civility and gentlemanliness, even making jokes and ensuring that everything Silas and I needed was attended to.

When we reached the ship, with its three other members still stationed aboard, Ambrose announced very loudly and confidently that he was stepping down as the captain of the MORAY and that Silas was going to take the lead to bring us home. Grant seemed skeptical, and I assumed him to be one of Ambrose's men, but Jacks and Goode were hardly fazed, more concerned with bringing aboard the treasure and supplies from the jollyboats, and we had no trouble amongst any of them. When asked what happened to the rest of the crew, the look from Ambrose was so dark and murderous that not another question was asked to him for the remainder of our berth.

Clark and Franklin, having escaped the massacre in the tent, were not seen again as we set sail away from that cursed island. To take them home for the gibbet would have been a cruel sort of kindness in any right. We left them a crate of supplies, and Silas said a prayer for them as the island retreated from view on the distant horizon.

After a thorough search of his cabin for any hidden weapons, Ambrose was restricted to his quarters, and a padlock and length of chain ensured that he could not slip out. For the first two days at sea, Silas delivered meals to Ambrose himself, but after that, he allowed me to bring him his bread and water.

The first time I came with it, he only took the meal with polite thanks before closing the door again. This repeated for nearly a week until we were far out to sea. I brought him his dinner, unlocking the door and setting the chain aside. Ambrose met me politely before asking, "Won't you join me for a few minutes, Jamie? It gets a power lonesome in here."

I gazed back at him, and he smiled. Not his usual silver smile, but something genuine and hopeful. "I promised you, no funny business. Just to talk, and I am unarmed."

I wanted to say no, and thought it might be wiser to do so, but I had not had a moment alone with Ambrose since he had rescued me from Roderick on the beach, and before that had been the trip into the jungle to retrieve the map. Despite the villainy he had wrought, my heart still fluttered at a look from him, and I found myself entering his familiar, warm quarters.

He sat in a chair, the same chair he had bent me over the first time on the ship we had joined together, and I knew I blushed as I sat down opposite him.

Ambrose smiled gently at me. "He's a good man, that Cross," he said. "Was always lookin' out for you, Jamie."

"He's a good friend," I said softly.

Ambrose nodded slowly, leaning forward with his elbows on his knees, his head bowed for a moment, before he said, "I will keep his secret about the men he killed."

"What?" I asked, after much too long of a pause.

Ambrose lifted his head and gave me a small smile. "You know he killed Madsen and Miller and Humbolt, don't pretend you don't."

I gazed back at him for a moment before asking, "But not that first night? Thatch and Vanders?"

Ambrose chuckled softly in his throat. "No. He was only adding fuel to the fire I set."

I gaped at him, my mouth hanging open. "You killed them?"

Ambrose nodded slowly. "I did. I intended to kill them all by the time we returned to England."

"Why?" I demanded, suddenly wondering if I had made a horrible mistake in sitting down with Captain Ambrose.

"Treasure does terrible things to people, Jamie. I'm sure you know that now as well as I." Ambrose rubbed thoughtfully at the scruff on his cheek. "It weren't rightly theirs anyway, and every last one of them scoundrels and rats of the sea. I curated them carefully." He chuckled softly. "Well, most of them. Obviously, I vastly underestimated your friend, Mister Cross."

Silas would probably be pleased with that assessment.

"From the day I brought him ashore, he was prepared that there might be a mutiny," Ambrose continued. "You were always his first priority, especially once he found out the squire and Kearns were dead."

"You used him to manipulate me," I pointed out.

"I did," Ambrose said softly. "It was a wretched thing for me to do, Jamie, I admit to that. But that Cross, he was brave, and no mistake. He knew I was the one killed Vanders and Thatch, and he could have ratted me out to the rest of the crew. But he also knew he could instead turn the crew against me while reducing their numbers, so that is what he did. And when he knew that there was talk of throwing me off, he made a bargain with me. To protect you."

I swallowed hard at this revelation. Silas had slain those men in the dead of night so he could make a deal with Ambrose, knowing that the man held me in his affections. All of those men were dead because of me. But yet, they still would have been dead before we returned to England if Ambrose's original plot had gone as planned. "So you changed sides again," said I.

"And make no mistake, I'll hang for it when we get back to port," Ambrose said softly. "I won't tell anyone what your friend did to save you." His dark eyes met mine, and I saw in them the man he had once been. A young man, perhaps just a bit naïve, looking for adventure, to carve out his own X in the world, to live and love and die. Things could have been so very different if he had not betrayed the squire or tried to bring harm to Silas.

Ambrose reached out and took my hand in his, grasping it gently. "I would never have hurt you, Jamie. I suppose that is the weakness in me, for all the blood I have spilled, but I meant every word when I said that I wanted you by my side."

Hot tears filled my eyes, but I would not let them fall. He was not worthy of my sorrow. I rose to my feet. "I never want to see you again, Mister Ambrose," I said softly.

Ambrose nodded and silently pressed a last kiss to the back of my knuckles. My heart ached, for I wanted him still, despite the treachery. He had saved me many times over, but I could not do the same for him. I walked out of his cabin and did not return again the rest of the voyage.

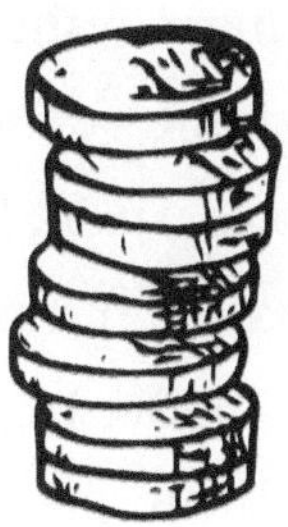

We were only days from home when Miles Ambrose, along with Bosun, disappeared. One of the jollyboats was missing, as were several large bags of gold and trinkets, only enough that one man could carry himself. Sitting on the chair in his quarters was the page from Morgan's Bible with its hastily scrawled black spot, my silver compass next to it. How he slipped from his quarters on the MORAY, I never did know, but slip he did, silently away in the night, laden with crimes and riches.

I was pleased to be so cheaply quit of him, and indeed, I was glad that he was gone. While he had done monstrous things, I still ached for the man who had befriended me, taken me into his bed, and saved me from death at risk of his own life. I could not bring myself to call it love, and I didn't think Ambrose would have called what he felt for me love either. But yearning still rose in my chest long after he was gone, and I was thankful I would not have to see him hung and gibbetted on Execution Dock for his crimes.

We reached port with no sign of the jollyboat or its traitorous occupant. The few remaining crew members were given an equal share of the treasure and used it wisely or foolishly, according to their natures. Silas accepted his share but told me he had "had enough of pirates fer a while, thank yeh very much," and I was more than happy to have him join me as I was suddenly left with the burden of settling Squire Harrington's affairs.

With no surviving captain or owner of the MORAY, it was left to me as the squire's designated heir to decide what to do with it. Too much blood had been shed on its decks for me to want to retain it, so I sold it and the antiquities shop to pay off the squire's debts. Then Silas and I traveled the European continent: Italy, Greece, Spain, France. He pursued his passion of cooking, and I pursued my love of history.

Upon our return to England, I moved to a fine townhouse in the nearby city of Wortherton. Silas stayed with me, as my cook and my friend. He did not ever have to work if he did not want to; he could have bought a king's castle with his share. But cooking was still his passion, and he was happy to have someone to share the experience with. I was grateful for his continued friendship and wealth of knowledge when it came to running my own household and assets.

I never knew what became of Captain Miles Ambrose Locke. I never heard from him or of him again. But once my heart had healed, I realized I was not sorry to see the last of him. My ability to trust was forever on edge because of the havoc wrought by his manipulations of me.

The fortune I amassed from that blood-soaked voyage was more than I could have ever imagined in my limited experience. Much of it became investments, some donations, and I lived in modest comfort with Silas for many years. Neighbors and friends came and went. I joined several gentlemen's clubs for travelers and scholars, and many of my associates enjoyed coming to our home to see what new creations Silas had put together. Our home was referred to as *Captain Cross's Kitchen*, which made Silas quite proud until he passed away some dozen years later after a bout with pneumonia.

Shortly before Silas took ill, I met a man by the name of Richard Arrow who was a down on his luck tutor of literature passing through town. We became fast friends, and I was glad to have him by my side when Silas passed on. After I had mourned my dear companion, Richard stayed on to help run my estate. Within months of that, we were lovers, and we have been together ever since. He taught me to trust my heart again, and his love is better than any treasure I might have ever found in any chest in the world.

Epilogue

Upon hearing my tale of adventure and swashbuckling, Richard commended it be written out for posterity, and, after much cajoling, I was unable to deny his request. So, here it is, laid out for you, full and complete in its retelling. I have declined to include details of the location, as it is possible there may still be treasure buried deep within that cursed jungle, and I will not be responsible for more lives lost in search of it. If one happens upon it, I have no desire to stake a claim, for my life is complete with my holdings and Richard at my side. I have burned the map with its coordinates.

The only paper I have remaining to corroborate my story is that curious page with its blackened circle, the only piece of Captain Miles Ambrose Locke I have left, and the only part of him I wish to keep. The black ash has smudged and faded now, into shades of gray, not unlike the man himself.

Once in a while, I imagine what might have been if I had accepted his offer to follow him into a life of luxury or buccaneering, where we might have ended up. We might have done a power of good together, or we might have danced a jig side by side at the end of a rope on Execution Dock. I will never know, but that suits me just as well. I may not be a "gentleman of fortune," but I am free to go wherever the wind may take me, with a man who truly loves me by my side. My life is rich with adventure, and that is worth its weight in gold.

About the Author

Kit Barrie (she/her) was raised by pirates in a traveling carnival where she learned how to fly and to weave fantasy into reality. She identifies as chaotic bisexual, with good intentions and questionable methods. She lives in an utterly unfantastical state in the Midwestern United States with her very supportive spouse (VSS) and at least 4 food goblins who might just be cats gobblin' food.

Please visit www.kitbarrie.com or scan the QR code below for more information on Kit and her other available titles.

www.ingramcontent.com/pod-product-compliance
Lightning Source LLC
Chambersburg PA
CBHW020652010826
48969CB00012B/796